VALENTINES FOR NURSE CLEO

Cleo had plenty to occupy her working on the Coronary Care Unit, trying to lose weight, give up smoking—and dreaming about the glamorous Sir Phineas Grimes. She didn't give much thought to Dr Tony Fitzgerald until a Valentine's Day prank put her in his bad books. Then she ran into him in very different circumstances. Would this be her chance to make a better impression on him? Apparently not, because now there was Angie Carruthers...

VALENTINES FOR NURSE CLEO

Valentines For Nurse Cleo

by
Lilian Darcy

Magna Large Print Books
Long Preston, North Yorkshire,
England.

British Library Cataloguing in Publication Data.

Darcy, Lilian
  Valentines for Nurse Cleo.

  A catalogue record for this book is
  available from the British Library

  ISBN 0-7505-1010-2

First published in Great Britain by Mills & Boon Ltd., 1987

Copyright © 1987 by Lilian Darcy

Published in Large Print June, 1996 by arrangement with
Harlequin Books SA.

Magna Large Print is an imprint of
Library Magna Books Ltd.
Printed and bound in Great Britain by
T.J. Press (Padstow) Ltd., Cornwall, PL28 8RW.

CHAPTER ONE

'You going off now, Nurse?' old Mrs
Rattigan wheezed cheerfully, as Staff Nurse
Cleo Fitzpatrick swung a warm navy cape
around her uniform-clad shoulders on her
way through Women's Medical.

'Yes, at last,' Cleo returned, firmly
stifling a sigh and the note of complaint
that had threatened to creep into her tone.
'I'm nearly an hour over time, and the
staff Christmas party is on tonight. I'll
have missed half the fun if I don't get
there soon... Not that our celebration on
the ward wasn't fun too.'

She added the last sentence hastily,
remembering how long Mrs Rattigan had
been here, and how unlikely it was that
her Christmas held much more promise of
good cheer.

'Yes, I had a whale of a time, I must
say,' Mrs Rattigan laughed. 'In spite of my
old chest.'

She suffered from severe emphysema,
but was surprisingly happy, and had earned
Cleo's respect more than once with her
courage and determined high spirits.

'You look after yourself, Mrs Rattigan,'

Cleo admonished her patient now, in her clear, bell-like voice. 'Tonight was my last shift on Women's Medical, and I'm not sure that I can trust anybody else to be half strict enough with you!'

A broad, friendly smile accompanied the teasing tone.

'Get away with you, you cheeky girl!' said Mrs Rattigan, and a younger patient in the next bed joined in the laughter, then spoke.

'I hope you enjoy the Coronary Care Unit, then, Nurse Fitzpatrick,' she said.

'I'm certainly hoping to,' Cleo replied, her blue eyes bright and alive. 'It'll be a challenge, at any rate.'

'Don't think about challenges for tonight,' advised Mrs Rattigan. 'Just enjoy the party.'

Cleo promised herself doubtfully that she would try to do so as she hurried off the ward, acknowledging the goodbyes and best wishes of several more patients with a smile and a wave of her hand. She was tired after beginning work at three, and it would be after midnight by the time she had freshened up, changed, and crossed from the nurses' home to the big staff dining-room where the party was being held.

The event would already be in top gear, and no doubt a few people would be more than a little under the weather. It might be hard to fit straight into the celebratory atmosphere. It would be different if she had someone special to go to the party with, as did so many of the other nurses...

This started a familiar train of thought in Cleo's head, and reduced her mood still further, so that by the time she reached her room in the nurses' home, she was almost thinking of not going to the party at all. A shower revived her, but the dress she chose to wear—a wide shouldered sheath style in pale silvery grey—was a distinct squeeze, confirming her fear that she had put on too much weight in the past couple of months.

It was eating canteen stodge three times a day, she told herself, refusing to take into consideration sundry cakes and pastries partaken of between meals. Her skin wasn't blemish-free at the moment, either...

Weakly she reached for the cigarettes that lay on her small bedside table. She had been thinking of trying to give up, but what the heck!

'Why even try to look after a body like mine?' the cynical words were spoken aloud to the empty room, but there was laughter and self-awareness in them.

And Cleo was being far too harsh on herself, of course. She was actually far from unattractive, and her physical faults loomed much larger in her own eyes than in those of anyone else. Softly-waving honey-gold hair, almost luminous blue eyes, and a pink and white complexion made her something of an English rose, and it was only recently that the full curves of her figure had expanded into plumpness, and her skin had lost its peach-like smoothness.

'Cleo Fitz, you're in a rut!' she said sternly to her reflection in the mirror, then poked her tongue out at it.

There was truth in the accusation, she knew—and she also knew that she was allowing herself to coast along with the realisation, frowning at that mirror daily, and continuing with less than positive thoughts.

Such as right now, for instance. She crossed the frost-covered lawn that separated the nurses' home from the staff dining-room with head bent towards the ground, shoulders sloping despondently, and face grimly reflecting her certainty that the evening would be a disaster. It wasn't an attitude that would encourage the blossoming of new relationships and exper-iences in her life.

As she had expected, the dining-hall was crowded and noisy, even without the rather loud rhythms of the dance band, who had just announced that they would be taking a brief break. Tables and chairs had been cleared to one side, and the pace seemed hectic. It was difficult to pluck up the courage to enter alone, and perhaps it would be minutes before she encountered a friend.

'But it's now or never, I suppose,' she muttered to herself, with a momentary surge of determination, then ducking her head as if in self-defence, she ploughed her way into the hall.

'Buck up, Cleo!' Miraculously, her best friend Jane pounced on her almost immediately and sized up her mood accurately and without hesitation. 'What's wrong?'

'Oh...nothing.'

'Oh...nothing,' mimicked Jane, exaggerating Cleo's tone until it became a moan of melodramatic proportions.

It had the desired effect, and Cleo's rich golden laugh bubbled up. She had a strong sense of humour, and small but mischievous Jane could almost always jog her out of a black mood. The problem was that they hadn't seemed to see much of each other lately, with Jane studying hard for her Midder, and their days off coinciding only rarely. Jane had been flat-sitting for her godmother for the past month too, and Cleo had missed their mealtime conversations and nightcaps of cocoa in the nurses' lounge.

'Sorry,' Cleo apologised now. 'I'll pull myself together, shall I?'

'Do,' Jane replied. 'But first tell me...is anything really wrong?'

'Oh, I don't know,' Cleo sighed, then quickly changed her expression to a bright smile of thanks as she accepted a glass of punch from a young orderly who was doing voluntary duty as a drinks waiter. 'I'm just wondering why I bothered to come to this bash, that's all.'

'Why?' asked Jane.

'Well, what's the point? What are these things for? To find a boyfriend—or to show off the one you already have.'

The last sentence was added in a *very* sour tone as a pretty—and very slender!—first-year nurse paraded past with a rather good-looking houseman in tow.

'Cleo! That's outrageous!' Jane responded with understandable astonishment. 'I've been having a wonderful time, and I didn't come for either of those reasons.'

'Didn't you?' Cleo probed lightly.

'Well...' Jane blushed prettily and tossed her light brown curls as Cleo nodded pointedly at a fair-haired physiotherapist who had been showing signs of returning Jane's shy interest lately.

'See what I mean?' Cleo was suddenly serious again. 'You're the only person in the world I'd say this to, and it's not as though it's the only thing that's important, by any means, but I do wish...'

She stopped after the rush of earnest words, finding it difficult to describe the need she was beginning to feel, even to her best friend.

'That you'd fall in love?' Jane finished for her gently.

'Not even that,' Cleo replied quickly. 'I'd just like to feel that there were some possibilities on the horizon, but no one's even asked me out for ages.'

'So you're just here to find a boyfriend too,' Jane ventured to tease.

'Yes, but I *won't* find one, that's what hurts,' Cleo retorted fiercely.

'I don't see why not,' said Jane.

'Look at me,' Cleo replied in a low tone. 'Overweight, my skin's a mess...'

'Not nearly as much as you think,' Jane consoled her. 'And you're a fabulous person, with your sense of humour. You've got tons of things going for you physically, too. Your hair, your eyes, your voice...'

'My *voice?*'

'You have a gorgeous voice, and that's a really attractive thing. Too many girls underestimate it,' said Jane with truth. 'Look at all the unattached men here tonight. There's bound to be one for you.'

15

'Now I'm beginning to feel as if I'm at a cattle market!' groaned Cleo theatrically.

'Rubbish! You just have to learn to—oh, relax a bit. You're loads of fun in the nurses' home, and you're always just about the most popular nurse on the ward. Try your hardest to think positive tonight, and see what happens,' advised Jane.

Just then the music started up again and conversation became too difficult. Cleo didn't want it to continue in any case. She wasn't a girl who liked to burden her friends with her own doubts and fears, and Jane was right. The best way to enjoy herself was to be determined to do so.

A bouncing and swaying mass of dancers had formed quickly now that the band was playing its last numbers of the evening, and Cleo decided to put down her empty glass and weave her way in amongst them to shake off the slight ache in her back that had come after a long day on the ward.

Unfortunately, she acted a little too quickly on this decision, and collided quite sharply with a tall stranger. He had a full glass in his hand and had not been attempting to dance, so the accident was entirely Cleo's fault. And it seemed quite typical of her appalling luck of late that every last drop of his beer should have cascaded down *his* front, instead of her own, making a spreading patch of dark

16

wetness all over what looked to be a rather expensive grey suit.

Cleo could only gasp ineffectually for several seconds, too mortified even to find any words of apology, let alone go and look for something with which to mop up the mess. Mercifully, Jane appeared on the scene again like a guardian angel, with a whole fistful of paper table napkins which she pressed into Cleo's distracted hands before the stranger had spoken. Feverishly, Cleo began to rub at the suit, but all that seemed to happen was that bits of green paper fluff adhered to the wetness and made more of a mess than before.

'Look, I'll do it, shall I?' The stranger spoke at last in a voice that contained the unmistakable trace of a Northern provincial accent, and it was only then that she realised he wasn't quite a stranger after all.

Her heart sank—or it would have done, if it had not already been lodged firmly in one of her shoes. She looked up. He was a tall man, strongly-built, and yes, she did recognise that face. Bluish eyes, fair clear skin with no tan, strong jaw. Someone had pointed it out in the canteen for her only the other day. Dr Tony Fitzgerald, native of Lancashire, and Registrar in the Coronary Care Unit where Cleo herself was due to start work in three days.

Limply she surrendered the wad of green paper and watched him press it carefully to the wettest parts of his suit with firm, efficient fingers. Sensibly, he didn't rub at it, and so didn't leave sticky threads of paper on the grey wool fabric as Cleo had done.

She noticed that his face was faintly flushed—probably with suppressed anger—and that his dark wavy hair was rumpled carelessly. He hadn't spoken since his offer to take over the mopping up, and in an attempt to make herself feel better, Cleo added this fact to a newly-manufactured list of reasons to dislike him. The man was boorish and rude. Why didn't he say that it was as much his fault as hers? That wasn't true, of course, but it would have been polite, unlike this grim silence.

He looked like the kind of person who was too accustomed to being in the right. He had an arrogantly prominent nose, wide shoulders, large capable limbs—*too* large, Cleo decided—and a chin that convinced you instantly that he had never spilt a drink down someone else's front in his life.

He straightened now—'pompously', she said to herself, although she knew the word wasn't accurate at all—and spoke again at last.

'Don't hang around,' he said. 'There's nothing you can do. I'll just have to let it dry off.'

'But the suit...'

'I'll get it dry-cleaned.'

'I'll pay...'

'Look, for heaven's sake, it wasn't your fault.'

Well, there was the polite reassurance Cleo had thought he should give, but it wasn't worded very fully, and perversely she allowed herself to be goaded into further speech.

'Actually, it *was* my fault, and I have no intention of shirking the responsibility. If you'll simply tell the dry-cleaner to make the bill out in my name, address care of the nurses'...'

'I don't have a pen and paper with me, I'm afraid,' he returned. 'And I would very much prefer to let the whole thing drop, actually.'

He turned away without waiting for her reply, holding the now-sticky wad of green gingerly, and obviously searching for some way to get rid of it. A moment later he had disappeared and the incident was over.

As far as Cleo was concerned, of course, the party was now an irrevocable disaster. Jane was nowhere to be found, and no one looked as though they were about to ask

Cleo for a dance. The band was playing a slow number now too, so bobbing about by oneself was out of the question.

She wandered out into the long passage that ran along the side of the dining-hall, and was immediately greeted by several friends from the nurses' home who seemed to have gathered for a gossip away from the din of the crowd and the music.

'Having a good time?' asked Shirley Byrne, moving further along the table on which she was perched, to allow Cleo some room.

'So-so,' Cleo replied.

Even this noncommittal statement erred on the side of optimism, but Shirley was a restless and rather blunt girl who was generally unsympathetic to other people's moods, so Cleo didn't bother to be truthful. In any case, they were by no means close friends.

'Picked up any dishy men?' asked another girl, Suzanne. The question reflected her own preoccupation with that activity.

'Not so far.' Again Cleo decided to make light of it.

'Shh!' exclaimed Shirley with a sudden giggle, as two pairs of heavy masculine feet were heard just around the corner.

'That's Dr Murdoch from Orthopaedics,' said Suzanne in a loud whisper, as the two men came into sight.

'And Dr Fitzgerald from Coronary Care,' added Shirley.

Cleo flinched, blushed and turned her head away. It was rude, but she didn't want to meet the eyes of the Registrar from the Coronary Care Unit again so soon after their recent disastrous encounter.

'Not leaving the party already, are you?' Suzanne asked the pair boldly.

'No, just bringing in more drinks.'

It was Tony Fitzgerald who spoke, in a quiet, deep voice that was actually quite pleasant on the ear. Cleo's sudden realisation of this fact surprised her, and without thinking, she looked up at him as he passed. Their eyes met for an instant. They were nice eyes—cool greyish-blue, with a thoughtful twinkle in their depths. He did not give even the flicker of a smile, however, and Cleo reminded herself of her earlier almost instant dislike.

Dr Murdoch had slowed his pace and was evidently quite prepared to stop and chat to the four lively nurses for a while, but Tony Fitzgerald spoke, quick and low.

'We'd better get back with that beer, John.'

'Yeah, sure, you're right.'

And so they walked on out of sight around the next bend in the corridor instead. Inevitably, as soon as they were out of earshot, pretty, dark-haired Suzanne began to assess their masculine potential.

'Dr Murdoch's a bit of a dish, but he's been going out with that gorgeous St Lucian physio in Orthopaedics for months now. And Tony Fitz...'

'Yes, what about him? Does he have a girlfriend?' asked Diane Trelawney, the nicest of the three nurses.

'I'm not sure whether he does or not,' said Shirley with a sudden mischievous grin. 'But I tell you what! He'd be perfect for our Cleo here.'

She burst into peals of laughter in which Cleo thought she detected a slightly cruel ring. She remembered one or two run-ins they'd had in the past, and queried suspiciously, 'Why would he be perfect for me?'

'Well, you've got a great precedent, for one thing.' Shirley was still laughing at a joke that nobody else understood yet. Diane and Suzanne were now both looking curious and ready to be highly amused.

'What do you mean, Shirley?' asked Suzanne.

'Their names, of course. Don't you remember Antony and Cleopatra? Great lovers of history, shaking the foundations of whole kingdoms with the force of their passion!' giggled Shirley. 'I bet Tony is short for Anthony, and Cleo...'

'Is *not* short for Cleopatra,' Cleo finished the sentence for her ferociously, amidst laughter from the other two. 'It's just plain Cleo, and why my parents chose it, I'll never know.'

'*And* their last names are both Fitz-something,' Diane put in triumphantly, unperturbed by Cleo's interjection.

'You're right though, Cleo,' Shirley added in a lower tone which her two friends missed. 'You and Cleopatra aren't in the same class at all!'

'Great love affairs have been based on less, Cleo,' teased Suzanne. All three of the girls were looking at Cleo, and she felt herself growing hot and uncomfortable.

In another mood and with different people, she would have been able to laugh too, but she wasn't feeling very good about herself tonight, and she sensed, in Shirley's attitude at least, something nastier than just teasing. As well, since she had just thoroughly made up her mind to dislike Tony Fitzgerald, it wasn't pleasant to have other people matching her up with him, even on such superficial grounds.

But what was Diane saying now, in more serious tones?

'It's not just your names, either. I think you'd have lots of things in common...'

'Are you starting to take this seriously,

Diane?' Shirley interjected.

'Why not?' returned Diane. 'Cleo needs a man. They've got similar personalities in lots of ways. Good senses of humour—Tony's always laughing about something, with his friends, anyway, and then—ouch!'

She broke off abruptly, having been jabbed suddenly in the ribs by Shirley as a signal that the doctor in question was on his way back with the beer. Tony Fitzgerald eyed the group expressionlessly and flushed darkly as if he could read their suppressed giggling and shuffles of guilt quite easily, and was angry about it. He said nothing, however.

Cleo's own face was a strong shade of brick, and she felt mortified. Had he heard any of that? Probably Diane hadn't meant to be unkind, but her words were like barbs for all that. 'Cleo needs a man.' Was that what everyone thought?

It wasn't out of friendliness that they had suggested Tony Fitzgerald, either. It was purely a matter of the coincidence of their names. And Cleo hadn't missed Shirley's rather nasty hint that the ancient Egyptian queen's legendary beauty made a laughable contrast with her own less than scintillating looks. Probably the girl didn't think Cleo had a chance of 'having an affair' with Tony at all, in spite of her joke.

'Going back for another dance, then, Cleo?' asked Suzanne, as Cleo slid off her perch on the table and started to walk down the corridor. Tears had begun to prick behind her eyes, but she blinked them resolutely away and turned back to the group, determined not to reveal that she was upset.

'Yes. I'm getting cold out here,' she said. 'This dress isn't very warm. What about you lot?'

There! Her voice sounded all right. Just a little higher-pitched than usual, perhaps. They would never know how they had hurt her.

'I'm going to have another fag first,' said Shirley, and the others decided they would sit with her while she did so.

Cleo wasn't sorry. She returned to the dining-hall where people were still packed like sardines and evidently having a good time. She saw Tony again, dancing with an attractive staff nurse from the renal unit. He moved surprisingly well. Many tall, strongly-built men were as unbending and awkward as letter pillars on the dance floor, but Dr Fitzgerald seemed at ease with his powerful body...

She suddenly became conscious that she had been staring at him far too frankly. He was quite a distance away, but someone else might notice and comment, and she had had to listen to too many comments about Tony Fitzgerald already this evening! Quickly she flicked her blue-eyed gaze away and resumed her survey of the other dancers.

Jane was nowhere to be seen, nor any men of Cleo's acquaintance who might conceivably have asked her to partner them on the floor. Was it worth staying?

She decided it was not. The evening had been ill-omened from the start, and in her experience, when that happened it was best just to go home to bed and hide under the blankets where mischievous fate couldn't get you any more.

With a faint smile at this piece of whimsy, Cleo turned towards the exit door, not looking ahead to where she was going for the second time that evening—and for the second time, this resulted in a sharp collision with a tall man in a grey suit. But it would be *too* dreadful if it was Tony again...

Cleo looked up quickly and fearfully, to meet a pair of haunting dark eyes set in a very tanned and very aristocratic-looking face.

'My dear, I'm most terribly sorry,' came a deep drawling voice that throbbed with concern. 'I do hope you're not hurt in any way.'

As he bent over her, she was aware of

a very heavy waft of scented but definitely masculine after-shave which practically overpowered her, and his fingers were firm but almost caressing against her upper arm. Anyone less like Tony Fitzgerald would be difficult to imagine!

'Yes...I mean no, thank you. I'm fine,' she managed to gasp in reply to his enquiry.

'Glad to hear it,' he murmured, as he trailed his hand lightly down her arm, touching her flesh below the elbow-length sleeves of her dress, and sending dangerous tingles through her.

She was faintly aware of several people hovering about this distinguished stranger, and wondered who they all were. Not that the rest of them were particularly important. It was just this man: his confident bearing, the silver-grey hair that actually made his face look younger, his aristocratic Roman nose. Not to mention the way his touch had thrilled her, and the way his apology had been so smooth and his concern for her so well expressed.

Cleo had to find out who he was. Could she possibly ask...? No, it was out of the question. The group was still standing about, some of its members a little awkward now, although the darkly tanned, silver-haired stranger still looked perfectly assured and at ease, as if he expected someone else to make the next move, and was quite content to wait until they did.

Cleo realised that she should go. It was gauche to keep standing here as if she expected to be asked to join the group, or apologised to again. Quickly she stepped away, after giving one last uncertain half-smile of thanks and apology, which she realised the tall man had not seen.

At that moment an older man approached, with long and somewhat anxious strides.

'Sir Phineas!'

'Miles... Good to see you!'

'I'm sorry, I got caught in a crush at the other end of the hall. This is your party? Come this way and we'll find you some drinks.'

The group moved off, shepherded rather fussily by Miles Gregson, the hospital's Director of Medical Administration. Cleo stood there, quite forgotten by them all, as was only to be expected. None of the party were aware that she was still watching them. She felt dazed.

Sir Phineas Grimes, the newly-appointed cardiothoracic surgeon at St Valentine's Hospital. Some people had been talking of nothing but this man for days, since his first professional visit only last week.

The nurses' home was alive with gossip about his looks, his social life, his recent separation from his wife of two years, the glamorous socialite Sabrina Tuckett-Ford.

And he had actually spoken to Cleo! Touched her, and seemed concerned. For a few moments Cleo thought about how Shirley would have boasted of the incident if it had happened to her. There was no danger of Cleo boasting about it, because she wasn't going to tell anyone at all. She was going to keep this experience to herself as a special memory...

Cleo took a last look at the surgeon as he walked confidently in the wake of Miles Gregson, surrounded by the five people who formed his entourage. A stunning-looking burgundy-haired woman in a low-cut shimmering black dress was at Sir Phineas's side, and as Cleo watched, he enfolded the woman's white shoulders with a long sensuous arm. Cleo felt a pang of quite surprising jealousy. She turned quickly and left the hall, dazedly wondering about the feeling. The whole complexion of the evening had been changed by what had happened during these last few minutes. Could it possibly mean anything? Was it the beginning of something important and new in her life?

CHAPTER TWO

'We're rather full at the moment,' Sister Hennessy frowned as she surveyed her domain from the raised and glassed-off nurses' station. Every bed but one of the eight-bed Coronary Care unit was occupied.

'I suppose Christmas has something to do with it,' hazarded Cleo, trying not to feel that her move from the relatively comfortable atmosphere of Women's Medical to this acute-care environment was a frightening one.

She had had three-month spells on Accident and Emergency during her second year of training, and on the ICU during her third, but this was the first time she had worked in such a pressure-filled area since qualifying, and she knew that more would be expected of her now. It was good, actually. It was what she needed. This conviction came firmly and suddenly as she listened to Sister Hennessy's reply.

'Yes, people just won't learn not to over-indulge at this time of year,' Sister was saying. 'Often even after they've had unmistakable warning symptoms already, too.'

She shook her head, as if this fact was simply incomprehensible to her. Aged about forty-five, she was thin to the point of angularity, and moved and spoke rather in the manner of a busy but chirpy little bird. Cleo felt a guilty moment of sympathy for the heart-attack-prone people Sister Hennessy was referring to, and a few cream cakes and cigarette packets floated across her inner vision.

'It isn't always so easy to give up your bad habits...' she murmured wryly, but Sister Hennessy didn't hear.

The nurses' station was rapidly becoming crowded as nursing staff gathered for the brief meeting that signalled the hand-over from night to day shift. On an acute-care ward such as this, the staff-to-patient ratio was one-to-one, and of course the Night Registrar would need to be here to speak to the Day Registrar if any problems had occurred during the night. That meant over a dozen people gathered together in what was not an enormous space.

Cleo sat nearest the door, next to Isobel Hennessy, who would be Sister in Charge of the coming shift, and who seemed like a pleasant enough person, in spite of being just a bit *too* brisk for Cleo's taste. While she continued to fill Cleo in on details

31

of ward routine as they waited for the Day Registrar's arrival, Cleo ventured a glance at the Sister's fob watch. Nine minutes past eight. The Day Registrar was a little late.

'It will be the first time you've met Dr Fitzgerald, I suppose.'

Cleo hastily returned her attention to the sister's words again as she caught the name.

'Mmm,' she nodded unthinkingly and a bit too brightly, to cover up the fact that her concentration had wandered for a few seconds.

'You'll like him, I think,' said Sister Hennessy. 'Although he does take a while to get to know.'

She added the last part after a faint pause, and with a sudden frown that had Cleo's curiosity and her apprehension aroused instantly. She had disliked him quite a lot during their disastrous encounter three days ago—at least, that was the impression that remained now—but she didn't really want to go on doing so. Disliking people didn't make working with them easy, so she hoped that the process of getting to know Tony Fitzgerald and, if Sister Hennessy was right, getting to like him didn't take *too* long.

She had her doubts, however, when she thought of how much the contrasting images of the two men she had met on Christmas Eve had stayed with her—Sir Phineas Grimes with his ready charm, after the cold aloofness of Dr Fitzgerald.

Several of the seven nurses on night shift were leaving now. Each of their patients, although very ill, had remained in a stable condition throughout the night, and the day staff who were replacing them were now adequately briefed. Cleo was just about to ask a fairly unimportant question about ward routine when a red light flashed on a panel on the desk, signalling that someone was outside the closed door waiting to gain entry to the ward.

For Cleo, this was another departure from what she was used to. Access to Women's Medical had been through open doors, but the patients in Coronary Care had to be protected from noise and unnecessary intrusion. The ward was well sound-proofed and its large wooden doors firmly shut against casual arrivals or noise from the corridors outside.

Sister Hennessy leaned quickly across to press the button that automatically released the door catch, and Cleo watched Tony Fitzgerald's entrance from the safety of the nurses' station.

He looked faintly harassed, as if it was already one of those days, and as he crossed the polished vinyl-tiled floor with long strides, he ran a large hand through hair that didn't require a further rumpling. Surprisingly, the untidy look suited him, and Cleo softened her feelings about him a fraction.

'Sorry I'm late,' he murmured to Sister Hennessy, his voice clipped and gravelly, no words wasted. 'Got tangled in a diagnostic debate.'

His eyes flicked over the other nurses, and he favoured Cleo with a small half-smile, as if he had the vague idea that he ought to know who she was. Cleo set her teeth and refused to smile back, her brief warmth towards him gone again. He was right! He *ought* to know who she was!

'That's all right,' Sister Hennessy was saying. 'Dr Morgan has left his notes. It was a quiet night, all things considered. He was only called in once, but he said he'd be in at about half past eight to fill you in further on that.'

Dr Fitzgerald nodded and read rapidly through the notes, his firm hand hovering over them with a pencil and marking a query or some cryptic letters every now and then. Immersed in work, he seemed self-assured, capable, and oblivious to anything else.

Cleo found herself idly studying the bone structure of his face. It was good, she decided dispassionately. Even planes to his cheeks, a firm jaw balancing a wide forehead. He was probably quite well aware of his good looks and build too. Perhaps he ought to realise, though, that there were many women who were quite capable of being immune to that kind of powerful physique—and she was rapidly coming to the conclusion that she was one of them.

A few minutes later the round began in earnest, and from then on Cleo was so caught up in the constant series of measuring, monitoring and charting procedures that form a large part of intensive patient care that she had little time to think of other things. She certainly forgot all about Tony Fitzgerald.

It was only when she had time to snatch a coffee at eleven that she was given a reason to think of him again. He had left the quietly busy ward after his round, to check on those patients whose conditions were now less critical, and who had therefore been moved to general wards, but had returned on an urgent summons from Sister Hennessy, when the patient in Bed Two had suddenly taken a turn for the worse. Now that he had revised his instructions on treatment, the Sister had persuaded him that he had earned a break too, and Cleo encountered him at the sink about to rinse a cup, as she was nimbly filling the electric kettle and preparing milk, sugar and cups.

'I'll make it. What would you like?' she asked cheerfully. It was an accepted part of a nurse's duties, and one which she often quite enjoyed.

The less stand-offish doctors usually made it the occasion for a friendly chat, while any who held misguided beliefs about the genetic inferiority of the nursing species could have their egos fed by being waited on and then left to themselves!

'Oh...er...whatever you're having,' Tony Fitzgerald murmured absently in reply to her question. He showed no further sign of recognising her as the person who had doused his suit on Christmas Eve, and his mind was still clearly on his work. But then he added in a helpful tone, 'Tea?'

'I'm having coffee, actually, but tea's no trouble. It's only bags,' said Cleo.

Again she spoke brightly, although she felt slightly uncomfortable at being shut away in this confined space with the man. It was only that his nearness reminded her too forcefully of the disaster of that spilled drink, she told herself.

'No, don't bother. Coffee's fine,' he replied, still absently, and loosening his tie a fraction, as he spoke.

'But honestly...'

'No, don't worry about it.'

'Because if you really do want tea—' Cleo persisted helpfully, switching on the exhaust fan and lighting a cigarette—her second for the day—as she spoke.

'Look!' His voice was suddenly resonant with irritation. 'I really don't give a tinker's cuss. I'll have coffee, and let's not keep pussyfooting around the subject.'

'Fine,' replied Cleo, with an edge to her voice that was only just acceptable when addressing a senior colleague. 'I didn't mean to pester.'

Another tiff over the subject of a drink!

'And do you really think the Coronary Care Unit is quite the place for cigarettes?' he added, frowning down at the offending object that dangled between her nicely-shaped fingers.

'It's permitted. There's a fan,' she said defensively.

'Permitted till the end of the year,' he reminded her. His grey-blue eyes were ice-cold, and narrowed in irritation. There seemed to be a deeper current to his anger too, as if he was struggling with some hidden emotion. It was disturbing. 'That's—what?—four days away. The regulations have changed, as you must know, and about time too. Although I suppose you think it's an infringement of your rights as a free human being to be forbidden to smoke near heart-attack patients.'

The last words came out as a cynical drawl, with only the faintest hint of humour, and for a moment Cleo was tempted to make a scathing retort, but then she pulled herself up short.

'No, I think you're absolutely right,' she said firmly. Her cheeks were burning, but her head was held high. She was determined to be honest, even in the face of this man's objectionable behaviour. 'Of course I wouldn't smoke if there wasn't a fan. In fact, I hardly ever smoke during working hours, only this is my first day on the ward, and... Anyway, I'm planning to give up altogether soon—at New Year, actually, maybe. In any case, wherever I am, I always refrain, *if* people ask *politely*.'

She had gone on far too much about it, but couldn't resist adding a last cutting phrase, although she knew she had already overstepped the mark. 'But I suppose you're still suffering from Christmas indigestion, so I'll make allowances for your rudeness.'

'Well, I'm certainly not suffering from Christmas good cheer,' he growled beneath a black frown. 'At least, not from some people. I think I'll skip the coffee, thanks.'

He glanced at Cleo's name-badge, as if noting it for future reference, pulled open the door of the tiny kitchen annexe, then stopped and wheeled around again, as if influenced by some new emotion.

Cleo suddenly felt absurdly frightened. What kind of an attack was this going to be? He had been about to leave and now he had changed his mind. It was evident that his anger was of the kind that was slow to surface into an eruption, but once it did...

Involuntarily, she shivered and her gaze flinched downwards.

With a precise click he had closed the door of the kitchen again, creating a feeling of claustrophobia and isolation. She saw that his strong fists were clenched, and that the rhythm of his breathing was deliberately steady.

'This isn't how I would have chosen to start a working relationship,' he said at last. 'And after that idiotic accident at the party too.'

So at least he *did* remember her face—although perhaps it would, after all, have been more flattering if he had not!

'It doesn't matter,' she said quickly, aware that for some reason she did not want to probe too deeply into the cause of the instant friction between them.

'It does, though.' He took a step closer to her, and she was aware of the masculine fragrance that hovered around his strong frame.

She knew that the movement was not a

threat, and yet she shied away from it. He noticed and stepped away again, making another visible effort to master himself. Cleo suddenly saw that the expression in his face was one of intense weariness and strain.

'You're tired.' The words were blurted thoughtlessly.

'Yes,' he said. 'So you'll have to forgive me if I'm saying this badly.'

'Forgive *you!*'

'Yes. Why? Were you about to apologise yourself?' He gave a sudden crooked grin that changed his whole face for a moment, softening its smooth well-chiselled planes.

'Actually, I was.'

It was true. Just in the last few seconds she had found herself ready for an apology, and had been about to meet whatever he said with an admission that he was quite right to reprimand her. Why was she finding it so difficult to control her emotions lately? She *had* been to blame, both at the party and this morning, and yet she had the most uncharacteristic need to put the fault on to this man instead of herself. It was the kind of thing Shirley Byrne would do, and Cleo was ashamed.

'Good. Well, let's take that as read, shall we?' Dr Fitzgerald was saying now. 'And if you'll accept my apology too, then perhaps we'll be able to get on to some reasonable footing. We have to—I believe that very strongly—in a place like Coronary Care. Don't you agree?'

The question shot out unexpectedly at the end, calling from her a stumbling acquiescence. He *was* a blunt man, and a laconic one. She was still trying to work out exactly what was so disturbing about him, when she became aware that he had gone, surprisingly silently for someone with such a strongly-built frame.

Cleo found that she was actually weak at the knees. That was supposed to be a symptom of falling in love, but in this case nothing could have been further from the truth, could it? This feeling was pure dislike, a clash of temperaments, negative chemistry. There had been that moment this morning as she had watched his entrance to the ward when she had thought his manner almost pleasant, but that had thoroughly gone now.

They rubbed each other up the wrong way, and that was that.

No, it wasn't, though, because she had just agreed with him that on an acute-care ward such as this one, it was important for staff to get on well together. Damn him! Why couldn't he have been someone benign and colourless and scarcely noticeable, instead of someone who confused her like this, and had her awash with three quite different emotions in as many minutes!

Abruptly but neatly, she stubbed her cigarette into the cheap tin ashtray she had placed on the sink, then took a hasty step across to prevent the electric kettle from short-circuiting in the sputtering water that spilled from its spout.

As she carefully rinsed out the ashtray and disposed of its contents, Cleo thought again of Shirley's facetious and slightly barbed suggestion that she and Tony Fitzgerald would be a good match. The memory of that episode had continued to smart rather painfully inside her over Christmas for several reasons.

Cleo's celebration had been very quiet this year. Her parents had gone bravely off to the wilds of north-west Canada, where Cleo's older sister Nancy led a rugged existence with her Canadian husband, running a holiday ranch and mountain trekking enterprise. Nancy had always been the flamboyant one.

Cleo's friend Jane had profited from the freedom given by flat-sitting and had organised a traditional turkey dinner for Cleo and two more of their nursing friends, who were lucky enough to be off duty, but had no families in London to go to. It had been fun to help with cooking, and to exchange presents, but not quite the same as a family affair, and when Stephanie and Lois had left to meet their boyfriends, and Jane had received an unexpected but clearly welcome phone call from the fair-haired physiotherapist, Cleo felt rather left out of things.

'Maybe I *should* try and get Tony Fitzgerald interested in me...'

It was ludicrous now to think that that thought had actually crossed her mind on Christmas afternoon. She had even mentioned the whole incident, including Shirley Byrne's comments, to Jane. She regretted it now, of course. What had Jane said?

'I hardly know him—he's not very big on the social scene. I think he works very hard. You could give it a go, I suppose.'

Not much of an encouragement, coming from one's best friend. Did Jane think he was out of her league too? And now this morning: his initial rudeness, then her own idiotic clumsiness and confusion. It would be best to forget all about it if she could, but it seemed like a bad omen for the New Year, and for life on Coronary Care.

Cleo made her coffee at last without much enjoyment, then her hands hovered hesitantly over the opened packet of sweet biscuits that sat invitingly on the buff-coloured laminex bench. Yes or no?

'These are *fattening*, Cleo Fitzpatrick!'

she reminded herself sternly.

But on the other hand, Tony Fitzgerald's behaviour had been very unsettling. Perhaps she really did need a pick-me-up. She took two biscuits.

'Nurse Fitzgerald?' It was Isobel Hennessy two minutes later, looking harassed.

'Fitzpatrick,' said Cleo automatically through her biscuit crumbs. Was this mistake going to be made with her name often on Coronary Care?

'Fitzpatrick, sorry, but quickly, we need coffee for Sir Phineas.'

'Sir Phineas! He's here?'

'Yes...the new patient in Bed Eight, Mr Sutton. I'm putting Nurse Leighton on Bed Six—Mr White—and transferring to Bed Eight myself. I must get back there. So...coffee.'

Cleo glanced quickly at her fob watch and was actually very surprised at the time. Her patient required quarter-hourly pulse readings for four hours following cardiac catheterisation, and it was only ten minutes since she had taken that last one, which had been quite satisfactory. The spat she had had with Dr Fitzgerald, and their subsequent awkward truce, had taken less time than she would have thought.

'He absolutely refuses to drink instant, though,' Isobel Hennessy was saying quickly, clearly anxious to get back to the great

44

man's side. 'He's liable to tip the stuff into the nearest kidney dish, apparently. Here—strong, black, no sugar.'

With nimble movements she opened a cupboard high on the wall, extracted a packet of expensive-looking ground coffee labelled 'Sir P. only', and a one-cup Pyrex jug and plunger, then darted back to the ward. Sister Hennessy's excited manner and the two spots of colour on her cheeks would have infected Cleo in any case, but in fact she didn't need anyone else to tell her that Sir Phineas's arrival was an event.

She felt quite strongly enough about it already, with no external promptings after her auspicious meeting with him on Christmas Eve. And now she was to make coffee for him!

Briefly, the thought crossed her mind that it wasn't necessary to get into *quite* such a state over this fact, but then she decided, very seriously as a nurse, that Sir Phineas Grimes was a busy and important man, and so naturally it was part of her duties to be as careful as possible over the delicate matter of his coffee.

Strong. Black. No sugar. She re-boiled the kettle, heated the small Pyrex jug, added a very liberal helping of coffee grounds, poured the boiling water on top, then left it to draw, her heart actually

45

hammering as she returned to the ward just in time for the next pulse reading. However, since Sir Phineas's patient was in Bed Eight and Cleo herself was fully involved with her patient, Stephen Cashman, in Bed Four on the opposite side of the ward, she could barely even see the great man.

Mr Cashman was very tired, as the catheterisation procedure had been long, although not especially painful, and he seemed drowsy now. Cleo smiled a little absently at him, her mind still on Sir Phineas. She could just hear his deep murmur across the ward.

'...Digoxin, i.v., point three...'

But now it was time to concentrate on Mr Cashman's pulse and ECG.

'Sister Hennessy!' Cleo's whisper was urgent. Isobel Hennessy turned away from her hovering position at Sir Phineas's side with a frown.

'Is it the coffee?'

'No—Mr Cashman. He's been fine till now, but there's suddenly arrhythmia in the last reading.'

'What's that?' Sir Phineas turned around, and Cleo received the full effect of his magnetic dark-eyed stare.

'Oh, not one of yours,' she stammered. 'Mr Cashman.'

'Yes, I know. Mr Cashman is a patient

of Dr Fitzgerald,' Sir Phineas nodded, smiling charmingly. 'But since he has just been called down to Post-op Recovery, and since he's rather a protégé of mine, I'm sure he wouldn't mind if I took a look at the problem. We've finished with Mr Sutton, haven't we, Sister?'

'Yes, sir. That is...everything seems clear.'

With almost feline grace Sir Phineas made his way to Bed Four, washed his hands and then proceeded to examine Mr Cashman. Sister Hennessy hovered about for a moment, but then she returned to her own patient, leaving Cleo to take meticulous notes of Sir Phineas's comments and prescriptions.

'Disopyramide, orally,' he said, and named a relatively low dosage. 'What's the possible side-effect there, Nurse? Can you tell me?'

'Retention of urine,' said Cleo, surprising herself with her promptness. The weakness in her knees which she had felt only minutes ago because of anger had returned, but this time the cause was very different. This man was gorgeous!

'Very good, Nurse.' ...And so charming in his manner! 'Make sure Dr Fitzgerald is told as soon as he returns to the ward, won't you?'

'Of course.'

'Tell him to page me if he has any queries. I'll be somewhere about for the next few hours.'

'Yes, Sir.'

'And now, I had the idea that someone was making me some coffee?' He favoured Cleo with a magnificent smile, revealing even white teeth.

'Yes, me, it was,' she replied ungrammatically, and virtually skidded into the tiny kitchen to squeeze the coffee grounds to the bottom of the jug with the plunger and pour out the dark liquid. Dark—it was practically black! Could he really like it that strong? What if she had made a terrible mistake?

'Excellent!' he said when she handed him the delicate white china cup—also specially reserved for 'Sir P.' 'It looks perfect.'

He turned from her and with tanned fingers drew a sheaf of notes towards him. Clearly it was a sign of dismissal, and Cleo returned to her patient, sternly telling herself that she could not afford to be flustered by his devastating attractions when there was vital work to be done.

But she felt in quite a glow, fresh and lively and aware in a way that she had not been for ages, it seemed. The day had suddenly taken a startling turn for the better.

Old Mr Sutton opened an eye as she went past, and Cleo caught his feeble murmur and faint smile, 'That's what we need, more pretty nurses...bit of spring in their step... Be better in no time with her around...'

Cleo was very tired when she left the ward at just after four. Her neat blue-striped but slightly too tight uniform felt stale, her feet ached, and her cap sat a little crookedly on her golden-blonde curls. Mr Cashman, an overweight man in his late fifties, was not an easy patient to care for. His condition was complicated by severe apprehension about the future, and his chances of leading a normal life, and Cleo's best combination of cheerfulness, mild teasing and concerned efficiency had not succeeded in reassuring him.

She did not despair, as she was naturally an optimistic girl—the only exception to this being her feelings of doubts about herself lately—and she was sure that by the time he was ready to go to the more relaxed atmosphere of a general ward, she would have managed to make some progress with him.

But it was tiring work. Tony Fitzgerald had nodded, frowned, rumpled his hair again and said very little on his return to the ward. Cleo had felt immediately tense, stiff and hostile, although he made no mention of their spat in the kitchen, nor of their subsequent awkward truce.

'Right. Just keep me informed, won't you?' had been about the extent of his chit-chat, before he had moved off again, leaving behind him the same faint masculine scent of after-shave and warmth, which she had noticed earlier and which she now found pleasant in spite of herself.

Perhaps because of this unwilling reaction, Cleo had poked out her tongue at his broad retreating back, muttered 'hatchet-face' under her breath, then had glanced quickly and very guiltily round the ward to make sure that no one had seen or heard. Very fortunately, no one had.

The epithet hadn't been quite fair, either. Tony Fitzgerald's eyebrows were strongly drawn and perhaps slightly darker than his hair, his lips were firm and his nose well defined, but he didn't really look much like a hatchet. Cleo might have liked his face—if she had liked *him!*

Still, in contrast to Sir Phineas Grimes's flawlessly tanned face with its smooth, ever-charming expression and the silver wings of hair at his temples which only made his appearance even more distinguished...well, there was simply no comparison.

A moment later Cleo decided she must have some mysterious power to conjure up the cardiothoracic consultant—simply by thinking of him, because there he was practically right in front of her. He was crossing the polished parquet floor of the large main foyer of the hospital, having emerged from a long corridor that mirrored the one Cleo had just left.

A quick calculation told her that unless he stopped for some reason, they would arrive at the large glass swing doors at almost exactly the same time.

'I *beg* your pardon!'

Of course Cleo had been so absorbed in Sir Phineas that she had not been looking where she was going and had scraped into a small, dumpy and irritable-looking woman who must have just arrived for afternoon visiting hours on one of the other wards.

'Yes—er—I'm terribly sorry,' Cleo murmured absently. It had only been a tiny jolt. She managed to get past the woman, then quickened her steps.

She had been a little careless, and she hadn't even apologised properly, which was unusual for her. The stern gaze of the hospital's Deputy Director of Nursing reached her. The senior nurse had obviously seen the visitor's annoyance while crossing the foyer herself, but Cleo didn't care. There would be a reprimand tomorrow, no doubt, but she *had* to get to the door before Sir Phineas so he would open it for her, and usher her through, and...

Rosy pink clouds blurred the picture at this point.

'Allow me...' It was happening!

'Thank you.'

Cleo slipped daintily through, then turned to smile up at Sir Phineas. She met a dazzling but somehow completely blank smile in return, and with a cold shock, realised that he didn't have the slightest idea who she was.

For a moment, this fact dashed all her hopes, but then she told herself that he had probably encountered hundreds of white-capped, blue-uniformed nurses since this morning, and probably millions of them had made coffee for him, so he couldn't be expected to remember her, with all the far more important things he had to think of. This reassurance did not completely comfort her, though.

It was sleeting outside, and a raw wind was driving the moist, stinging flakes almost horizontally. After the air-conditioned atmosphere of the hospital, the change was like a slap in the face. Cleo shrugged the regulation St Valentine's navy wool coat quickly on to her arms and over her shoulders, buttoning every button and retrieving matching gloves from her pockets, but she was still cold. The coat had a hood, but without ties it blew straight off her head again in a wind like this, and below her knees, her legs were protected only by thin stockings.

Sir Phineas wasn't bothering to put on a coat, although he carried one. In a moment Cleo saw why. In a small row of specially reserved parking places stood a gleaming dark-green Bentley, and while Cleo was still staring unhappily at the dark scudding clouds and the violently whipping black branches of the bare trees that lined the short hospital driveway, Sir Phineas had climbed into the car's sheltered and spacious interior and was starting the engine.

Quickly Cleo began to hurry along the footpath, deliberately exaggerating her hunched shoulders and lowered head. He would see her, pity her, stop the car, and...

With a rich purr the Bentley cruised past, its driver looking straight ahead, so that his aristocratic profile was silhouetted for a moment against the dull light of the late afternoon. He showed no sign whatsoever of slowing down.

Well, it had been a silly idea. Cleo noticed that there were half a dozen nurses at intervals along the path ahead of her. Why on earth should Sir Phineas stop for her and not them? Nurses were practically another species, and she had about as much chance as a snowball in a furnace of ever attracting any special attention from him. Her heart sank despondently, then she shivered. Speaking of snowballs...

She quickened her steps once more, unaware of another car that had pulled out of another reserved parking area shortly after the Bentley. Tony Fitzgerald drove a modest Japanese model which was somewhat less smooth in its acceleration than Sir Phineas's vehicle. The brakes squealed a little as the car slowed too. The noise drew Cleo's attention just as the Registrar from Coronary Care stopped and leaned across to wind down the window.

'Need a lift?'

'I'm just going to the bus stop, thanks, so it seems a bit pointless.'

She summoned a smile. This must be part of his attempt to find a working basis for their professional relationship on the ward, but he didn't really expect her to accept the lift. It was just a gesture.

'Fair enough.' He smiled too, briefly and formally, and had moved off again before she could even thank him for the offer.

Still, at least it had been a civil exchange, and there had been an awareness in the depths of his blue-grey eyes that she would recognise his offer as a further flag of truce.

'Fair enough.' She echoed his expression in her mind, and then a bitter gust of wind tore around the corner of one of the buildings and blew the incident from her mind.

'How was the first day, then?' Jane greeted her with the friendly enquiry half an hour later when Cleo turned up, blue and bedraggled, on the doorstep of the flat. They were to eat a nice non-fattening home-cooked meal together, to make the most of Jane's last two weeks of flat-sitting, then planned to go to a film.

'Fine...terrible...don't ask yet,' said Cleo through chattering teeth. 'I felt like Scott of the Antarctic walking up from the bus. Could I have a bath?'

'Of course you can, you poor lamb!' Jane exclaimed. 'Look at you, you're positively purple! Come in. I hadn't realised it was so ghastly out there. It's so cosy in this little flat. I've just been sewing and studying and listening to records all day. I haven't even poked my nose out the door. Here, there's bubbles, and lavender oil...'

Jane had wasted no time, but had literally dragged Cleo to the bathroom and was now filling the small apartment with steam as she ran the water at full pelt, adding liberal doses of bubble-bath and scent, and searching out a fluffy blue towel, that matched the well-planned décor of the bathroom.

'Your godmother has gorgeous taste,' Cleo observed from beneath the towel as she rubbed at her still-dripping hair.

'I know. And very sensible ideas about human comfort too,' nodded Jane. 'That towel must be about six feet square, and so thick! Hey, listen, shall I bring you a hot chocolate to drink while you're in there?'

'That's not very good for the circulation, is it?' It was fattening as well.

'I'm a nurse too, remember. I'm not running the bath too hot. It won't matter. I'll have one too, and we can chat in here while you recline in state beneath the foam.'

She nipped out of the steam-filled room to make the drinks, while Cleo lowered herself into the frothy, scented water with a sigh of bliss. Life suddenly seemed a much rosier thing, and the calorie-count of chocolate and milk unimportant.

'Now, Fitz, the details.'

The unashamed gossip session that followed was thoroughly enjoyed by both. Cleo gave full vent to her confused and uneasy dislike of Tony Fitzgerald, with which Jane was now prepared to be completely sympathetic. She also mentioned

Sir Phineas Grimes, of course, although she was by no means as honest about *him*. In fact, she kept quite quiet about his devastating effect on her heartbeat and knee-muscles, and was quite casual in her questions about him.

'He's broken up from his second wife, hasn't he?' she asked.

'Third, apparently,' replied Jane off-handedly.

'Third!'

That was a bit of a shock. A succession of short-lived marriages was more the style of glamorous film stars, Cleo considered. A doctor should be steadier, more sure of himself and what he wanted. Still, people could have bad luck. Maybe it had been entirely the woman's fault each time.

'And *are* you going to give up smoking at New Year?' asked Jane, changing the subject with this reference to Cleo's rash statement to Tony.

'Well...I really do want to give up,' replied Cleo, aware that she felt very much like a cigarette right at this moment. 'Just one day on Coronary Care has made me realise all over again how silly and harmful it is. And I'd hate to think I looked like Shirley Byrne does when she smokes, blowing affected little smoke rings all over everyone. It shouldn't be that hard to stop. I only smoke about fifteen a day.

But maybe not quite yet. "New Year" just slipped out before I thought—resolutions and all that, you know. But I mean, I've just started on a much more stressful ward. Maybe I need the old nicotine to wind down each day until I get used to the new routine.'

'Cleo!' scolded her friend. 'You'll never give up if you go on finding excuses like that.'

'I know...'

'Why don't you set a definite date for it, perhaps not New Year, but some time in a month or two, just try to cut down gradually till then, and then on that date, give up for good.'

'It's easy for you. You've never smoked.'

'No, and golly, am I glad when I look at people like you struggling to stop,' said Jane. 'But am I being a nag?'

'No... Well, yes, but I probably need to be nagged,' admitted Cleo.

'Okay then, name the day!'

'It sounds as if you're suggesting a wedding,' Cleo laughed.

'It does a bit,' Jane smiled back. 'So make it February the fourteenth—Valentine's Day. That's auspicious and romantic enough, and a tribute to the hospital. Maybe as well as stopping smoking, you'll start something really new that day.'

'That's a good idea, actually,' said Cleo

meditatively. 'It's not just smoking you see. There are lots of things I want to start and stop doing. Like *eating!* Cakes, I mean. And I need to exercise...'

'Should I be writing this down?'

'Writing it down?'

'With the heading "New Year's Resolutions". I'm not sure if I'd have enough paper, though.'

'Creep!' Cleo flicked a few drops of the now-cooling bath-water at her friend.

'I think it's about time you got out of there,' said Jane sternly. 'But hang on... What did you bring to wear? I don't remember seeing...'

'Oh no!' Cleo clapped a hand over her mouth. 'I completely forgot. I came in my uniform and I've got nothing else. I meant to call in and pick something up from my room, but instead...'

Instead, she had been far too busy mooning over Sir Phineas's dark eyes and silvery hair, and had absently wandered on to the bus without even considering her change of clothes.

'Don't worry, I'll lend you that dark green dress of mine, the one you wore once last winter, remember? And shoes are no problem. Our feet are the same size.'

'Thanks, Jane.'

Cleo was relieved. The idea of putting on her soiled and soaking uniform again and trekking back to the hospital in this weather did *not* appeal. Jane fetched the dress and left Cleo alone to dry herself and put it on.

It was a drop-waisted style in a rich green fabric of an unusual weave which imparted a glossy sheen to it. Shoulder pads, not too big, gave it a dressy tailored look, and with a matching silver and jade necklace and smart suede boots which Jane also generously offered, the ensemble would be a joy to wear.

There was only one problem: it didn't fit any more. Cleo pulled and struggled, determined to get it on, but terrified of ripping the seams. Finally she was safely in it, but her hips had padded out over the past year, and the drop waist, which was designed to fit snugly, just wouldn't sit on them at all, but kept riding up to her waist. It looked quite ridiculous.

'How's it going?' Jane popped her head around the door again. 'Oh.'

'Yes, impossible, isn't it?' Cleo said stonily. 'I'll be a complete dumpling soon.'

'But last winter...'

'I know.'

The old brown floral dress that Jane dredged up as a replacement just wasn't flattering, and it spoiled Cleo's entire evening. The meal was delicious, it was true—a chicken casserole with lightly steamed vegetables. But the film, a very popular romantic comedy and one which Cleo had expected to thoroughly enjoy, left a sour taste. Jane liked it, but Cleo found that she just couldn't identify with the heroine—she was far too slim and pretty!—and the likelihood of anything dramatic happening to change *her* life, the way it did in the film, seemed so remote as to be laughable.

CHAPTER THREE

St Valentine's Day was now approaching rapidly. Cleo was very aware of the fact, and though she groaned exaggeratedly about it to Jane, she was secretly looking forward to the date, and felt quite determined that it really was going to mark a change. The winter was proving a harsh one, and many tempers at the hospital were frayed. Struggling out of a warm bed to answer an emergency call, or arriving at work at eleven or midnight to begin a night shift, seemed even more difficult than usual. What was worse, the catering contract from the staff dining-room had been transferred to a new firm just after New Year, and the quality of meals had taken a decided down-turn.

Cleo was reminded of this by Dr Tony Fitzgerald after she had hurried hungrily into the noisy and rather stuffy canteen for a late midday meal one snowy and blustery Tuesday. Not that he spoke to her directly. He never did that, except when it was necessary on the ward—which unfortunately was far too often for her taste. But today he happened to be sitting with a group of friends at a table just near where the queue for meal trays began. Naturally, Cleo pretended not to have seen him—it was by unworded mutual agreement—and stared intently at a red and black printed notice about fire regulations which she must have seen at least five hundred times before. She recognised his undeniably attractive voice, however, with its rhythmic and almost lilting provincial accent.

'This steak and kidney's damn-well *grey*,' he pronounced disgustedly.

'And we could send the dumplings across to Orthopaedics—I hear they're low on plaster,' someone else quipped, amidst general laughter.

'Pity the poor blighters that live in,' Tony Fitzgerald returned. 'At least we don't have to eat this kind of stuff three times a day.'

The queue shuffled forward just then, taking Cleo out of earshot of Tony

Fitzgerald's table, and a moment later two more nurses joined the end of it.

'Hi, Clee!' One of them was Shirley Byrne, using a shortening of Cleo's name that she had always detested.

'Hullo, Shirley,' she returned politely, but not very warmly, since she didn't like Shirley much, and had good reason to suspect that the feeling was mutual.

'Sit with us?' Shirley's companion, Gina Woodley—a staff nurse on Obstetrics and a much nicer girl—issued the invitation, so Cleo accepted. Neither Jane nor any of her other special friends seemed to be about anywhere.

The three nurses received their own servings of the grey and unappetising stodge, then Shirley led the way, to Cleo's horror, to Tony Fitzgeraid's table. What a horrible coincidence!

A moment later she realised that the choice of table had been quite deliberate.

'Hi, Tony! Look who I've brought for you. Aren't you pleased?' Shirley said cheerfully, sliding into the seat opposite him and indicating Cleo.

His friends all seemed to be gone now, and Gina sat next to Shirley, which left Cleo with only one option—to sit beside the taciturn Registrar.

'Nurse Fitzpatrick.'

'Dr Fitzgerald.'

The greetings were mumbled. They had met already today on the ward, of course, so Shirley's opening remark was quite ridiculous and Tony Fitzgerald was clearly annoyed by it.

So was Cleo. But before she could think of anything to say to salvage the situation, Shirley had opened her large mouth again.

'Don't tell me you still call each other by your surnames! How primitive! And talk about shutting the door in destiny's face!'

Tony Fitzgerald just smiled politely at this and didn't rise to Shirley's bait. In fact, Cleo realised, he was not really listening to the sharp-featured nurse at all, clearly preoccupied with his own doubtless more important thoughts. It was a relief. Obviously Shirley wanted to repeat that silly joke about their names, but she wouldn't do it with so little encouragement.

The sharp-faced girl was looking across the table at the objects of her intended wit, and Gina was waving to some friends across the other side of the dining-hall. This had the strange affect of suddenly linking Cleo and Tony in shared embarrassment. Their eyes met fleetingly and for Cleo there was a strange sense of recognition when her blue gaze linked with his.

But the moment did not last long.

'Nice to have seen you, anyway,' the Cardiac Registrar said politely but distantly as he got to his feet and picked up his only half-emptied tray. 'Sorry, I have to...'

Then he was gone, striding over to the used crockery table and on out the door, rumpling his hair with a large hand—a gesture that was now very familiar to Cleo. She wished she could have followed him.

'Well!' exclaimed Shirley. 'Good manners, I *don't* think!'

'Come on, Shirley, said Gina impatiently. 'Didn't you see how tired he looked? Apparently he studies amazingly hard. He wants to go for Part Two of his FRCS exams this year, and he's much younger than average for that level.'

'I didn't know that,' Cleo put in, then was suddenly surprised at her own interest. She really didn't like him, and in the six weeks since the inauspicious start to their relationship, they'd barely exchanged a word that wasn't related exclusively to work.

However, she certainly didn't want to side with Shirley against him, and had felt quite sympathetic to his obvious feeling of irritation at the dark-haired nurse's intrusion on his peaceful lunch.

'Oh yes, he's being groomed for greatness,' Shirley was saying waspishly now. 'He's Phinny-baby's pet, didn't you know?'

'Don't call Sir Phineas that!'

The words were out before Cleo could stop herself. She bit her lip. It was a dead giveaway of the special feeling she cherished for the distinguished consultant.

'Why not?' Shirley retorted.

'It's...disrespectful,' replied Cleo lamely. A lot of girls used far worse nicknames for senior members of staff behind their backs, and Cleo let some of them slip at times herself after a particularly hard day. 'Phinny-baby' could be considered quite mild.

'You're just too good to be true, Cleo Fitzpatrick,' sniffed Shirley, evidently believing the reason she had given, but clearly scornful of it.

She ignored Cleo after that, and chattered one-sidedly with Gina, who gave Cleo a sidelong smile of sympathy before devoting her attention to Shirley. It was quite easy to finish the unappetising meal in silence. There were plenty of other things to occupy her thoughts.

Mostly daydreams, it had to be admitted —plans for new clothes to show off the slim shape she intended to have by spring, diet details to map out, ways she would get over her craving for cigarettes after she had stopped in just a few days' time.

And then of course the reward for all this. Would Sir Phineas at last notice her?

He noticed her already in a way, it was true. He spoke to her on average at least twice a week, usually to thank her for his coffee, and smile his overwhelming smile.

But Cleo doubted if he'd be able to identify her in a police line-up if his life depended on it—unless she happened to be the only one in a nurse's uniform. Still, it was bound to take a long time to make an impression on someone as distinguished as Sir Phineas Grimes.

'You don't seem a bit grateful for my matchmaking skills, by the way, Cleo.' Shirley leaned across the table and tapped her arm just as she was finishing her meal.

'Sorry?'

'I *said* you don't seem a bit grateful for me trying to match you up with Tony Fitz,' Shirley repeated crossly.

'I didn't find that joke funny in the first place, and I certainly don't now,' replied Cleo, her tone sounding more mild than she felt.

'Well, it *was just* a joke,' said Shirley defensively. 'I thought you'd quite enjoy it since you don't have a boyfriend, but some people have no sense of humour.'

'Having a boyfriend doesn't particularly concern me at the moment,' said Cleo, not quite truthfully. She decided to ignore the dig about her sense of humour. 'And it doesn't concern you either. When I do want one, I'll find my own, thanks.'

She got up, straightened her skirt and left, aware that she had sounded too snaky, but believing it was the only way to make Shirley let the whole thing drop.

Unfortunately, later events showed it to have been very much the wrong approach.

Things were quiet back on the ward. Four of the patients had visitors, including her own Bed Three man, Samuel Weldon. On a ward like this, visiting times were very quiet. One woman sat murmuring softly about family news to her husband. A daughter sat at her father's bedside and did nothing but pat his hand reassuringly at intervals and smile gently at him.

Mrs Weldon was holding her husband's hand, and they were both quite motionless. He was a lovely man. Cleo had decided that immediately four days ago when he had been brought in, and had found no reason to change her mind since. Aged sixty-eight, he was still in business for himself, running a small but moderately successful wholesale fabric warehouse in a light industrial zone a few miles from the hospital.

He was the type that never puts on weight, and Cleo could easily imagine his wiry birdlike form darting nimbly around the echoing warehouse as he gave orders and assisted customers, a pencil tucked forgotten behind one ear. He would have been well suited to the work, but business can mean stress, and stress can take its toll in heart disease.

At rest, with eyes closed, his face had fallen into grey old lines, and Cleo could see Mrs Weldon looking at it in miserable anxiety, clearly wondering how her Sam could have aged so much in such a short time.

'I'm afraid it's time for me to make some checks,' Cleo said quietly to the woman as she approached the bed. It was awful to have to interrupt like this. She saw Mr Weldon squeeze his wife's hand, and caught the firmer answering pressure she gave in reply too. 'It won't take long.'

'It's all right, dear,' Mrs Weldon said. 'If it'll help to make him well.'

Cleo went about her work as gently as she could, wishing that nurses could sometimes be invisible, or that they didn't have to stick so rigidly to doctors' instructions as to 'quarter-hourly' and 'hourly'. Mr and Mrs Weldon had a good marriage. It was one of those things that you could sometimes read very easily, just from the way two people sat or looked at each other.

Mrs Weldon's hair and complexion looked a little faded now—she must be in her mid-sixties—but once she would have been very pretty, with laughing blue eyes, wavy fair hair and delicate lips. Now the lips trembled a little, and Cleo felt a lump in her own throat at the sight of them.

Quickly she finished her routine so that the couple could be left alone again, but to her surprise as she left the bedside to enter up Mr Weldon's details in his file, she saw that Mrs Weldon had risen from her position.

'Nurse...?'

Sister Hennessy looked up from her own post two beds down and caught Cleo's eyes, sending a clear message: She needs you.

'Come with me somewhere where we can talk, Mrs Weldon,' Cleo invited.

'Is there somewhere? Do you have time?' The tone contained the threat of tears.

'Of course I do. And what about some tea?'

'No, it's all right.'

'There's a little room just out here.'

Cleo led the way out of the closed ward and along the corridor to a small carpeted space containing three or four easy chairs, a pot plant and a framed print or two, that served as a counselling room for three of the wards on this floor. She held the door open for Mrs Weldon, flipped a sign to read 'Occupied' and then they were alone.

'I just don't know what to do, I just don't know what to do,' Mrs Weldon began, then stopped as silent sobs choked her.

Cleo's heart went out to her, but she said nothing for the moment, and soon the small woman had regained some control.

'I'm sorry... It's just that I feel so helpless!' She managed a pale smile. 'It's silly really. That's all I want—something more I can do.'

'You're doing quite a bit already,' Cleo pointed out gently. 'You're coming in twice a day, and you and your son are running the business.'

'Oh, and that's not all,' Mrs Weldon laughed, dabbing at her eyes with a tissue. 'You should see the house! Spick and span from top to bottom. You could eat a meal off the back porch floor. I don't know why. I just seem to need to be doing something all the time, and really it's only that I want to be doing something for my Sam, something to tell him I love him, and I can't think what.'

'He knows you love him,' said Cleo, feeling the inadequacy of the words even as she spoke them.

'Yes, but I want to say it and not...not just in words. Oh, I'm so silly...' She stopped again.

'Yes, I see what you mean,' Cleo nodded slowly.

There was a faint discreet tap at the door.

'Nurse Fitzpatrick?'

She jumped up efficiently as she recognised Tony Fitzgerald's voice, and opened the door a little, her cheeks growing a little pink as she remembered the embarrassing moment they had shared over lunch because of Shirley.

'Isobel said Mrs Weldon was with you and might have some questions for me.' His voice was cool and quiet.

'Come in,' Cleo nodded brightly. 'I'm not sure if...'

'Oh, doctor, it's just me being silly. Not something you need to worry over,' Mrs Weldon told him.

'Let's hear about it anyway.'

He came carefully into the room, and Cleo saw that he had brought tea things on a tray. Unusual for a man in his position to do so. Probably Sister Hennessy had suggested and prepared it. Mrs Weldon took one of the steaming cups gratefully, and pressed her hands around it, using the gesture to still the trembling in her fingers. Clearly, she was again finding it difficult to think of the right words, so Cleo stepped in hesitantly.

'I...I think what Mrs Weldon is trying

to say is that...' She stopped abruptly as she caught a sudden frown from Tony Fitzgerald flicked in her direction, and felt stupid and clumsy and angry all at once. She had been trying to help!

Then she saw that Mrs Weldon was frowning too in her effort to put into words what it was that she was feeling, and realised that any other person's interpretation, no matter how sensitively given, was bound not to be quite right. Tony had known this.

'I want...to do something that he can see,' the older woman said at last. 'Something romantic like he'd do for me when we were courting...like huge armfuls of flowers...only not that, because everyone does flowers at a hospital.'

She paused, but neither Tony nor Cleo spoke.

'He's always been very romantic,' she went on. 'Even though you might not think it to look at him. Do you know, we've been married for forty-six years, and every one of those years—and the year we were engaged—we've given each other a Valentine card. We haven't missed one year, and we've kept every one of those cards, and every year they've been different. I just bought mine from a card shop, I'm not artistic, but Sam, he makes them himself, spends hours of it. Of course

I always have an idea that he's making it, one evening in February when he shuts himself away, but it's still as much of a surprise to see the cards all beautifully decorated...'

She trailed off again, but this time her eyes were shining with the memory, and Cleo was smiling too. So was Tony Fitzgerald.

'Mrs Weldon...' he began.

'Oh, I'm awfully sorry, doctor.' Her face was stricken again suddenly. 'How terrible to be wasting your time like this with my foolish old stories...'

'Not a waste at all,' replied Tony. 'Because it's given me a very good idea.'

Cleo looked at him curiously, her head tilted to one side. There was mischief in his tone, and it was echoed in the blue-grey depths of his eyes. For once she had completely forgotten her dislike of him and was simply interested in what he was about to say.

'I'm having your husband transferred to a general ward the day after tomorrow. If you could go home and find all those cards and bring them in, we could have them strung up on the wall behind his new bed, all ready for when he was moved. Would that be the answer?'

'That would be marvellous! Oh yes!' Mrs Weldon was laughing and her cheeks actually glowed with spots of pretty colour. 'Is it really possible?'

'Of course it is. We doctors are not complete ogres, you know,' he smiled. 'Just bring them in the day after tomorrow...'

'The day after tomorrow. I've lost all track of time since Sam was taken ill...'

'It's the fourteenth, Mrs Weldon,' put in Cleo delightedly 'The fourteenth of February.'

'Oh, it is too! Oh, how wonderful you've both been!' exclaimed Mrs Weldon.

'It was all Dr Fitzgerald's idea,' Cleo replied quickly, feeling scarcely able to take the credit.

'No! It's both of you. You could so easily have made me feel like just a foolish old woman, and instead...oh, it's exactly what I wanted, instead of all that silly house-cleaning...like the flowers, only...'

'Only *right*,' Tony finished for her.

'Yes,' she said. 'It's all *right*.'

'And it'll probably do him more good than any of Dr Fitzgerald's medicines,' put in Cleo daringly.

'No doubt it will,' he returned, apparently not at all put out by the idea.

'Oh, thank you again. I'll just say goodbye to my Sam, and go home and get out all the cards straight away, and I'll bring in string and Sellotape...'

The little woman scarcely waited to finish

her sentence, but was already stepping along the corridor back to the ward. This was probably just as well, because by this time Cleo could not contain her delighted laughter, and Tony, surprisingly, seemed to be similarly affected. For several seconds they just stood there, then Cleo recovered herself.

'That was all she wanted—a vibrant, romantic way to tell him she loved him. How lovely to be able to take the weight off someone's mind so quickly and easily, and in such a delightful way. It's one of the times that make it all worthwhile, isn't it?' she said.

'Are those times so rare for you?' He was serious again suddenly.

'No, I didn't mean that, but...' she trailed off.

'No, I know you didn't.'

'I'm glad you came in, because I wouldn't have thought of the idea,' said Cleo, looking up at him again and for once feeling able to meet his grey-blue gaze.

She almost wished they could keep talking for a few minutes, because next time they met it would be bound to be fraught with suppressed hostility again. It was only these special circumstances which made it different.

But of course he would have to go, and so should she. There was a moment of silence that seemed to be suspended out of time, while a strange current of awareness passed between them, almost as if... But then:

'Yes... Yes, it was good.' Tony rumpled his hair with a large, capable hand, chuckled and grinned once more, then was gone, leaving only a tiny hint of the familiar scent of his after-shave.

'I can't wait until the day after tomorrow to see the cards!' Cleo called after him, but the words trailed off as she realised he was already out of hearing range.

How funny that they should have got on so well for those few moments, and then that last feeling of awareness and recognition. Perhaps it would signal the start of a more relaxing working relationship...?

It didn't.

CHAPTER FOUR

St Valentine's Day didn't begin too badly. The weather was comparatively mild, and steady if pale and wintry sunshine streamed into Cleo's room. She was on a B shift that day, and was luxuriating in the warmth of her bed, having decided to skip breakfast

77

and laze away half the morning with a book, which was turning out to be excellent.

Nurses' rooms at St Valentine's Hospital were small and took a bit of getting used to if you'd moved in there at seventeen straight from a comfortable family home, as Cleo had. After over four years, though, she didn't think about the pale murky green of the walls any more, and had exchanged the scratchy regulation blankets for a crimson-covered duvet that she loved.

It was now nearly ten, however, and probably time to think about getting up. The idea of a cigarette crossed her mind, then crossed back again, then just floated wistfully about.

No, not any more! Be firm!

She still had an almost-full packet in her bottom drawer, as it happened, because someone had told her that it was worse if you religiously got rid of them all. When they were out of reach, they became an obsession, aparently. They were certainly not an obsession already, Cleo told herself.

But she leant out of bed weakly and reached towards the drawer.

Then she thought of the new patient who had died in Bed Two yesterday, with Tony Fitzgerald issuing urgent instructions as he worked over the man, trying to massage and shock the heart back into life. And she thought of the man's wife who had been visiting at the time, standing white-faced and numb in the background. The patient in Bed Two, only in his early forties, had been a self-confessed 'sixty-a-day man'.

The drawer stayed shut, and she kept thinking of Tony Fitzgerald instead. You never really forgave yourself for a patient's death. Cleo couldn't forget how Tony's hands had been shaking when he had finally given up and turned to Mrs Goodwin.

'I'm sorry.' That was all he had said, but his tone had carried something in it—a sincerity and commitment that Cleo had had to admire, just as she had had to admire his solution to Mrs Weldon's problem.

He had ruined it all an hour later, of course, by some boorish criticism of a minute aspect of her charting procedures, stopping by her table in the canteen as she was sitting back with a well-earned after-dinner cup of tea. This just went to show that it was wise to take no notice of moments that seemed special. The day-to-day reality of their work together on the ward was what told the truth about their feelings towards each other, and she would *not* forget it again!

An excited knock at the door sounded hard upon this firm decision.

'Cleo, are you in?' It was Jane.

'Come in. It's not locked,' called Cleo, and a moment later her friend had bounced into the room.

'Look! I was passing the letter-rack, and...Cleo, it's for you, and it's *got* to be a Valentine!'

'No...' She shook her head, but her heart had skipped a beat all the same. Valentines were certainly in everybody's minds this year.

She had toyed with the idea of sending one to Sir Phineas Grimes—anonymously, of course—but at the last minute she had decided not to. Could he possibly have had the same idea, though? Perhaps he had noticed her after all? But she abandoned the foolish notion straight away. She had outgrown that kind of fantasy long ago.

'Your fingers have gone all fluttery,' commented Jane. 'It is a card, isn't it?'

'I th-think so,' said Cleo, her teeth chattering a little. Was it excitement, or just cold? Now that she was sitting up in bed, the pink floral cotton nightie she wore didn't offer much protection.

'For heaven's sake, hurry up,' Jane was saying. 'I'm dying of curiosity. Maybe some gorgeous guy has been madly in love with you for months and...'

She broke off as she saw Cleo's stony face, and snatched at the card. Cleo handed it over dully. It didn't matter. It wasn't important. But for some reason she felt sullied by it, especially after the Weldons and their forty-seven years of romance.

The card was pink, with a heart of silver glitter that had a shiny red arrow through it. Inside, the printed message had been neatly painted over with white-out, and some lines written in, in an exaggerated Roman-style script.

'"My heart is to thy rudder tied by strings, and thou shouldst tow me after." I don't get it.'

'It's a quotation from *Antony and Cleopatra,* I presume,' replied Cleo.

'Shirley Byrne?'

'Obviously.'

'Why?'

'She's still on with that stupid joke about our names. I told her the other day that I didn't think it was funny. I don't know if she honestly thinks it is, or if she's really trying to hurt me in some way—she's never liked me. Did you read the next bit?'

'Yes,' nodded Jane. 'I wouldn't read *that* aloud. It's going a darn sight too far in my opinion—not funny, just bloody rude. Look, just ignore the whole thing. Don't even mention it to anyone. If she hints about it, pretend you never got the card,' she suggested. 'That's quite plausible with the delivery service around here. It's not that important, is it?'

'No, I know. It's silly to be upset.' With the back of her hand, Cleo wiped away a couple of tears that had somehow dropped on to her thick lower lashes. 'I wouldn't be, except that I don't even *like* Tony Fitzgerald, Shirley knows it. That's why she's doing it.'

'Sounds almost like a vendetta.'

'It might be,' Cleo agreed. 'Remember in first year when I went out with that houseman from ENT for a while? I didn't realise until afterwards, but he was an ex of hers, and I think she blamed me for the break-up.'

'But that's ridiculous! That was years ago, and it wasn't your fault anyway. James Hickson used to go out with a million girls a week until he met Nicola Naseby and discovered true love. And that wasn't until last year,' said Jane indignantly.

'I know.' Cleo overlooked her friend's ever-so-slight exaggeration as to the number of girls. 'But Shirley and I have rubbed each other up the wrong way a few times since as well.'

'You wouldn't do a thing like that to her, though, would you? Specially that last sentence,' Jane said passionately. 'You don't hold grudges like that. It's all her. Just forget it—it doesn't matter. It's over.'

But it wasn't over, although Cleo didn't find that out for some time.

'Do you know, I hate living in this place,' Jane was continuing. 'It makes people like Shirley all the more poisonous. I think we've been here much too long.'

'You mean...?'

'I've been feeling this ever since I moved back from Aunt Louise's—I had such a great time there. We should both move out of the nurses' home. It's so *restricted* here!'

Jane was still speaking rapidly and heatedly as she was sometimes wont to do. Cleo could only listen in silence, still smarting over Shirley's unpleasant trick in spite of Jane's advice to forget it.

'I don't just mean because of rules and regulations, although there are enough of those, with Matron still living in the Dark Ages. I can't see nearly as much of David as I'd like to...' At this Jane smiled and flushed faintly. David was the fair-haired physiotherapist she had been interested in for so long, and it was obvious that something serious was developing there. 'But it's restricting our whole growth. We were still kids when we moved in here. Now we're women, trained, responsible, capable, and we need to...to...'

Here her eloquence failed her, but Cleo was nodding, as well as laughing at her friend's earnest and firebrand manner.

'I do know what you mean,' she said, sitting up further in the bed and gathering her legs up underneath her. 'But is it possible? You mean we share a place?'

'Yes, why not?'

'Can we afford it? We can't go too far from the hospital, we need a bedroom each, with our different hours—not to mention privacy!—and a decent living area, and we don't want anything totally grotty. Otherwise we're better off here.'

'We'll have to look. It might take months, or maybe we'll have to go in with other people. We mustn't rush into it, but I do think it's the right idea,' Jane enthused.

'Yes...'

Thinking about it cured the sting left by Shirley Byrne's Valentine, anyway, and when Cleo went to work at four, after what she hoped would become a regular swimming session at the local indoor pool, she realised that she hadn't thought about reaching for a cigarette even once.

On her way out of the nurses' home, she saw that the second post had come, and that once again there was something for her. *Not* another Valentine. Instead, a printed, official-looking envelope which was sure to be boring. There was no time to find out now, though, so she folded it hastily and stuffed it into her coat pocket, before hurrying out into the late afternoon with an anticipatory shiver. It was still clear, but there had been a cold snap and tonight there would be a heavy frost.

After seven weeks in the Coronary Care Unit, many things were now second nature to Cleo—checking ECGs automatically each time she walked past a monitor, taking hourly rhythm strips and BP every four hours. She had become used to this intensive level of patient care, and used to the fact that although there were several other nurses on each shift, they rarely had time to talk to each other much. She was used, as well, to the fact that most patients only stayed a few days before moving either to surgery and the ICU or to a general medical or surgical ward when their condition improved.

The second afternoon visiting hour was just ending when Cleo arrived. She had been assigned to Bed Six now that Mr Weldon had gone to the general ward, and was soon fully involved in her work there, after the previous nurse had departed.

Brian Rickett was relatively young—only thirty-seven—but was planning to run for Parliament at the next elections and had been under a lot of stress as he rushed around at a hectic pace 'making myself visible in the constituency', as he phrased it over-smoothly to Cleo. This afternoon he was, as usual, obsessively meticulous about observing doctors' and nurses' orders, so as to be fit and able to return to normal life as soon as possible, but when Cleo suggested gently that perhaps he didn't have quite the necessary stamina for a political career his reply was interesting, to say the least.

'Oh, once I'm elected I won't have to bother with it,' he pronounced impatiently.

Cleo glanced at his notes: 'Profession: Used-car dealer.'

'And is that your attitude to after-sales service as well?' she asked wickedly, then jumped as a low chuckle broke out directly behind her. It was Dr Fitzgerald, who had approached without her noticing.

'Certainly not! Rickett's Motors, best after-sales service in the district!' Mr Rickett spluttered pompously, and Cleo felt a little guilty. In his condition, he shouldn't be excited in any way.

'I'm sorry, it was a joke,' she said, as she took her first set of readings for the day.

She glanced anxiously at Tony Fitzgerald, too. He had laughed on the spur of the moment—she was beginning to suspect that he did have a sense of humour, at least!—but perhaps he would be angry at the fact that his patient had been disturbed.

He stood at the foot of the bed leafing through Mr Rickett's notes, and there was certainly a wry expression on his face, but he didn't look angry. A few minutes later, when she was recording some details on the Kardex at the raised nursing station, he came over.

'You didn't know Amiodarone was a truth drug, did you?' A crooked half-grin accompanied the words. 'I doubt if he's ever been so honest about his political intentions before!'

'I'm sure he hasn't.' Cleo laughed her rich golden laugh, enjoying the joke. Amiodarone was the relatively new heart drug Brian Rickett was on. 'You'll have to write a paper on it, or an article for the *BMJ*. Your reputation will be assured for life!'

They exchanged another smile—which must make it one of the most amicable few minutes they had ever spent together, Cleo thought, coming a close second to the other day's laughter in the counselling room. But then Tony Fitzgerald continued to stand there, although she had bent her head over her notes again, and it began to unsettle her. She looked up enquiringly a minute later. Did he want something? Why didn't he say so?

He seemed to sense her uncertainty and impatience. 'Angie Carruthers has been on this ward for quite some months now, hasn't she?'

'Oh—er—yes, I believe so,' answered Cleo. Sister Carruthers was a stunningly attractive brunette who so far had mostly been rostered on different shifts from Cleo. 'But I myself haven't been here for very long. I would have thought that you'd have a better idea of when she came to Coronary Care.'

'Oh yes, it's just that—well, frankly, I'm a little surprised,' explained Tony, frowning. 'I've just taken a look at Mr Rickett. His condition is quite satisfactory, and yet Angie paged me just before she went off, to report that she was worried about him. I didn't get here till after she'd left, as you know, but it's the third time in two weeks that she's done something of the sort.'

'Perhaps she had a bad experience with a patient recently, made some kind of mistake, and it's rocked her confidence,' suggested Cleo, surprised that he had spoken of this to her.

'Perhaps,' he said, very absently, and it was suddenly clear that he had been speaking his thoughts aloud, rather than truly looking for Cleo's help. Irritated, although she didn't quite know why, Cleo returned to her Kardex.

With his determination to be 'cured'

as quickly as was humanly possible, Brian Rickett did not make an easy patient. He was obsessively concerned with the minutiae of his condition, and was constantly calling Cleo's attention to tiny and meaningless 'symptoms'—a twitching eyelid, cold toes, one lone sneeze. He was really quite ill, and Cleo was surprised that he had the energy to be so inquisitive about his body.

She found the constant reassurance and investigations she had to make quite draining in addition to the complicated and regular series of more vital tasks, and it was quite a relief when she could go off for a quick evening meal.

First she popped downstairs to Ward 6A where Mr Weldon now was. There was no need to do so, it wasn't usual for a nurse from Coronary Care to visit a patient once he or she had been moved, but Cleo just couldn't resist having a look at those Valentine cards.

It didn't take long to find the right bed, and there they were, exactly ninety-four on the wall behind, and one—this year's gift from Mrs Weldon—on the table beside him. Mr Weldon himself seemed like a different man. He was actually sitting up in bed, and the grey old colour in his face was gone.

Of course he wouldn't be allowed to feel

too energetic just yet, but it was clear that the festive appearance of the cards, such a visible token of his wife's love, had brought about a considerable change.

'Hullo, Nurse,' he said, as Cleo approached. 'Come to take a look? Go ahead!'

'They're beautiful, Mr Weldon,' she said sincerely, examining some of the cards he had made himself. They were arranged alternately with the printed cards and went year by year. Some were delicate pen-and-wash drawings, others slyly amusing collages cut from magazines or photos, some had glitter and stars, others had sequins and ribbons, and all were done with exquisite delicacy and care.

'I'm the most popular man on the ward with these,' the old man said. 'All the doctors stop and take a look.'

'I'm not surprised.'

'Dr Fitzgerald was in about half an hour ago...'

'Was he?' Oddly, Cleo was sorry she had missed him. Only because they could share part of the credit for this display, of course.

'He looked at every single card.'

'That was nice of him. I wish I could, but if I don't go and eat now, I'll be late back on the ward.'

'Come again, if you like,' he invited.

'I might do that.'

She examined one more card and then left, a tinge of wistful sadness threading through her soul as she took a last look at Mr Weldon and the display from the doorway. She herself had received a Valentine. Oh yes! That travesty of a joke from Shirley Byrne. Much worse than receiving nothing at all...

It was only as Cleo put on her coat to cross the open area that separated the main building from the staff dining-room at she heard the crackle of paper in her pocket and remembered the unopened letter she had received earlier. None of her particular friends seemed to be around, so she sat at a table by herself and opened the thick envelope.

Startled, she recognised the letterhead of her father's solicitor, but it was only with slight sadness that she read of her great-aunt Marjorie's death in far-off New Zealand. She could only remember meeting the old lady once, when Cleo herself had been about five years old, so her lack of real grief was quite understandable.

The really surprising part was that Great-aunt Marjorie seemed to have left her seven hundred pounds!

The old lady must have had several other great-nieces and nephews, not to mention various other relatives, although she had never married or had children of her own, so it seemed that she had spread her legacies widely. Or perhaps the fact that she had been a nurse for over forty years had something to do with it, as Cleo was the only other member of the clan to have followed that profession.

Whatever the reason, it was a very welcome surprise. Cleo spent a few minutes thinking over what she knew about the old lady. She must have been well over eighty, and had probably been rather lonely in her old age, but she had led a full life, and according to the solicitor's letter, the new gynaecological ward at her old hospital in Wellington was to be named after her, an event which had given the former Matron a great deal of pleasure and pride during the last months of her life.

The next thing to think about, of course, was the money. Cleo was so busy with this activity that she chewed her way through an impossibly leathery chop, with vegetables to match, without even noticing.

Seven hundred pounds. It wasn't a lot these days. Not enough to invest or save for anything really big and special. It wouldn't even buy much of a car—though no doubt the shifty Mr Rickett would have something 'just right for you, and a genuine bargain' in his yard. But on

92

the other hand, it was far too much to simply fritter away on clothes and outings and oddments.

It was no good trying to think of what Aunt Marjorie might have wanted, either. Cleo hadn't the slightest idea. Had she been a penny-pincher? Or would she have wanted her great-niece to splash out in some special way? Still, there was no rush to decide anything.

It seemed like some kind of a sign from Fate, though. The very day she had given up smoking and begun to put her new health plan into action, the very day she and Jane had thought of moving out of the nurses' home, a windfall like that came along out of the blue! Perhaps it meant that she should spend it on health and fitness somehow, or on furnishings for a new flat.

It wasn't until the next day that she had any more concrete ideas, however.

'Come for a walk with me this afternoon?' said Jane over lunch in the staff dining-room. Once again, both girls were on an afternoon shift.

'In this?' Cleo made a face at the long windows that ran the length of the dining-room.

It was blustery and freezing cold. A change had come during the night—Cleo had woken at the sound of heavy rain and felt that bed was the most delicious place in the whole world—and it did not look as though the weather would clear today. Although at this precise moment it was not raining, brief heavy showers clattered suddenly down every half hour or so, and it scarcely seemed like the day to go hunting up the first hints of spring!

'Why not?' queried Jane. 'You look as though you need to get out. If we put on every woolly and waterproof garment we've got, it could be fun.'

'It would be nice to get out, I must admit,' Cleo nodded.

She had spent the morning writing letters and studying up on a few aspects of coronary care which she had realised were too hazy in her memory. At times, the temptation to reach for a cigarette to go with the steaming mug of coffee at her elbow was almost irresistible. Once, in fact, she had actually lit one up and drawn in a long heady lungful of tar and nicotine, listening guiltily all the while for footsteps that might stop outside her door. If Jane or Mandy or Gail caught her after all her vows...! Then this furtive attitude had seemed so stupid. She couldn't hide a stolen cigarette from herself, and it was for herself that she was giving up, so she had stubbed it out again after only a few puffs.

But there were still sixteen left in the packet in the drawer, and when lunch-time arrived to take her mind off the problem, it had been an incredible relief.

'Where shall we go, then?' Jane was asking.

'Oh, through the park...watch the ducks trying to chip through the ice on the pond,' teased Cleo. 'Then why not do some shopping—Jane!'

She broke off abruptly as she realised that she hadn't even told her friend about the seven hundred pounds yet.

Of course, remembering about this added a whole new dimension to the expedition. Cleo covered her smoky blue corduroy pants and black angora pullover with a knee-length navy coat in an anorak style that was both padded and waterproof. She added a matching wool cloche hat that came well down over her ears, navy wool gloves, a fluffy white scarf and shiny black Wellingtons, which hugged her well-shaped calves and managed to look almost elegant.

'I'm much more of a rag-bag,' laughed Jane as she looked at her friend's get-up. It had to be admitted that she was right. Yellow plastic raincoat, pink Wellingtons, scarlet gloves and a green hat and scarf swamped Jane's small person with colour.

'Well, if we get caught in a blizzard on

our way through the park, which seems quite likely, the rescue party won't have much trouble finding us,' Cleo said. 'And at least you look slim.'

'Are you kidding? I'm wearing about six pullovers under this!'

'So it's through the park, first stop the bank, then you're going to help me spend a bit of money. Agreed?'

'Yes,' nodded Jane. 'And then estate agents to look for a flat, and at that rate we'll probably be jolly lucky to be back in time for work.'

Although St Valentine's was located in an outer part of London, it was close to a local conglomeration of shops and services, where practically anything could be bought or ordered. Happily for the medical staff, who were often tied to the concrete and glass jungle of the hospital for days at a stretch by oddly-arranged duty rosters, the way to the shopping area was via a large, wild-looking park. It made a nice change, even though as Cleo had said, at this time of year there was little beauty or activity to observe, apart from some ducks who appeared to be as heartily sick of winter as were most human beings.

The two girls traversed the park at a brisk pace, daydreaming aloud about the flat they might find this very afternoon, and arriving at the bank with glowing cheeks and well-exercised lungs.

Cleo was sensible and only took out a little bit of money. Legal paperwork took time, and it might be a while before the money actually came through. However, after a year on staff nurse's pay, with her only holidays spent cheaply at her parents' home in Devon, Cleo's bank balance was healthy, and she could actually afford to spend the whole seven hundred pounds before it even arrived.

'What are you going to get?' asked Jane. 'A blouse? A dress? Jeans?'

'No,' replied Cleo firmly. 'Because I *absolutely* intend to lose weight—in fact I've lost a bit already—so I'm not going to buy anything like that until I'm back to good old size twelve.'

They left the warmth of the bank building and braved the windy street once again. Cleo was busy putting her money safely away in her purse, so she didn't notice the dark-green car which pulled smoothly into a newly-vacated parking space just along from the bank.

'Ooh, Cleo, look! Isn't that Sir Phineas Grimes?' whispered Jane, interested. Cleo took a quick look at the car. She'd even memorised the number-plate by now.

'Yes,' she answered, and blushed a shade of beetroot as the Bentley's owner stepped out, adjusted the astrakhan collar of his perfectly-fitting black coat and strode briskly in the direction of the bank. He had to pass the two girls quite closely, as a harassed mother with a toddler and a pram was blocking most of the footpath at that point.

In a rare moment of mad audacity, Cleo smiled brilliantly at the great man, and opened her mouth for a polite 'Hullo, Sir.' Surely he must recognise her by now! But the corners of his slightly too full lips lifted only faintly as he brushed past, and the words died before she had uttered them. Her face fell.

'What's the matter?' asked Jane.

'Don't you think he's gorgeous!' The words were out before she thought, accompanied by a heartfelt sigh.

'Sir P.? Yes, I suppose he is. I hadn't thought about it before,' was Jane's careless reply.

'Hadn't you? I think about it all the time,' Cleo confessed, deciding that she might as well give the whole game away.

'Do you?' Jane said. 'I suppose you see him a fair bit on your ward.' Down in Obstetrics, Jane was far removed from the great man's sphere.

'Yes, several times a week if I'm lucky. He's fabulous... Do you think I've got any chance with him?' Cleo stopped in her

98

tracks and grasped her friend's plastic-covered arm beseechingly.

'Well, hardly,' Jane screwed up her slightly freckled face apologetically, 'since he didn't even seem to recognise you. It might be different if you were glamorous and gorgeous like Angie Carruthers—she's on CCU with you, isn't she?'

'Yes, you're right,' said Cleo gloomily. 'All his wives have been super-gorgeous, *and* lusciously dark. Maybe if I got my hair dyed...?'

'Cleopotamus!' Only Jane could get away with this outrageous nickname, coined one hilarious night two years back.

'Am I being silly?'

'Yes!'

Cleo knew she was, and didn't say anything more about the cardio-thoracic consultant, but deep down a defiant little voice insisted that she shouldn't give up hope. Stranger things had happened. If they could get to know each other, they might have a lot in common, and if her diet and exercise régime went well... Just imagine riding round in that Bentley for the rest of her days!

A man's car was perhaps not a strong base for a lasting relationship, but dreams have the advantage of blurring these small details.

'What about this place? I've found some

great things here over the past couple of years.' Jane had stopped outside a dim, mirrored and fashionable boutique that sold mainly shoes and accessories such as jewellery, scarves, and headgear.

Cleo shut the door firmly on the compartment of her mind labelled 'Sir Phineas Grimes' and concentrated on the spending of money instead. She emerged from the boutique quite some time later with a long floating scarf of Wedgwood blue silk, a pair of low-heeled shoes in rich chestnut leather, and two pieces of glittering costume jewellery.

'Not very extravagant at all,' said Jane, who had been an invaluable help during the entire exercise.

'I know,' Cleo nodded 'I don't want to just blow it on clothes, you see. I'd like to do something really *satisfying* with the money, and maybe even have something left to put down the deposit on our flat when we find it.

'A Mediterranean cruise?' Jane suggested.

They stopped, not for the first time in their lives, outside the travel agent's window.

'Are you kidding?' shrieked Cleo. 'Look how they advertise them! Pictures of enormous shipboard banquets, and then flaking out on deck in the sun all day like a piece of blubber. I'm supposed to be losing weight and getting exercise, not turning into a walrus!'

'True.' Jane pushed a wayward lock of pale brown hair back under the hood of her raincoat and frowned.

'But a holiday is certainly an idea,' Cleo agreed.

'Let's go in,' suggested Jane. 'I'm freezing! Let's sit down cosily and see what they've got to offer.'

The travel agency was full of tantalising posters of faraway places: temples in Greece, Amazonian jungles, tropical beaches of white coral sands...

'Can I help you?' a benign-looking young man queried as they stood awkwardly in the carpeted centre of the office.

'We're not sure,' said Jane, but suddenly Cleo found she knew quite a lot about what she wanted. They sat down and she ticked off a list on her fingers.

'I'd like something not *too* expensive—I don't care about luxury. Something fairly energetic. A week or so. Not sightseeing, but staying in one place, out of England...'

'Whew! Stop there,' laughed the young man. Francis Trewes was his name, according to a name-badge he wore. 'By energetic, did you mean sporty?'

'Possibly,' Cleo replied.

'Because in fact it's the ideal time of year for skiing holidays. Would that fulfil your requirements?'

Skiing! Cleo had certainly never even considered the idea before.

'Tell me about it,' was her cautious comment, after an audible gasp from Jane.

'Well, for a start I'm sure it would cost less than you think. It's low season in France from the beginning of March, and we always recommend Skimmer's Tours, which organise literally everything for you. By air to Geneva, then bus to Les Deux Aiguilles...'

He outlined the entire holiday, and Cleo surprised herself completely by getting more interested in the idea every minute. Jane suppressed a giggle at her side, and when Mr Trewes went away to get some pamphlets, she murmured in Cleo's ear, 'Don't waste the poor man's time, love.'

'I'm not,' said Cleo at once, and it was at that instant that she made up her mind. 'Don't you believe that I'm really changing my life-style?'

Of course I do, but skiing's a bit extreme, isn't it?' Jane wrinkled her daintily freckled nose. 'You've never done anything like that before.'

'So? Thousands of people do it. Fifty million Frenchmen can't be wrong, or whatever it is. I'm going to try it.'

Jane sat back in sheer admiration.

'Cleo Fitzpatrick! You are sometimes

the most surprising and wonderful person! Good for you!'

In just a few days the whole thing had been organised. Cleo was to leave on the holiday in less than two weeks. She had applied for leave and obtained it easily, as she had three weeks owing to her. Mr Trewes had given her a list of special clothing requirements, her passport was in order, and it was all going to happen. Sometimes Cleo had to pinch herself to make sure she was still real.

The girls had been less lucky with flats, however. The estate agent had looked a little amused when they had described what they were looking for.

'How far are you prepared to travel?' he asked them.

'Not far. We're nurses at St Valentine's Hospital, and we have odd hours,' Jane had explained, and the portly agent had leaned across his desk and stared at her coldly.

'Then I really think we're wasting each other's time,' were his crisp words. 'The market is very tight at the moment, and I doubt very much that anything is going to become available in your price range, given the features you seem to require. Perhaps you'd better go away and think about it more realistically.'

'Nasty man!' Jane said when they were safely out the door.

'Positive creep,' agreed Cleo—which helped to vent her feelings, but didn't get them any closer to finding a place to live. And if they really were being unrealistic...

'If only we could afford somewhere like Aunt Louise's,' sighed Jane, not for the first time, over dinner one Friday night.

Actually, it wasn't just any Friday night in Cleo's eyes, but *the* Friday night, the day before she was to leave for the holiday which was now causing flutters of trepidation as well as excitement inside her.

'So will you keep looking while I'm away?' she asked.

'I suppose so. Although the other three agents I've been to all said the same as that first horrid man. They must know what they're talking about. I knew it would be hard, but I didn't think they'd all be *quite* so discouraging!' Jane frowned, making one of her cross elf-like faces.

'Anyway, I've got to get back,' said Cleo, suddenly noticing the time.

'I won't see you before you go, then?' Jane grasped her friend's arm.

'No, I'm off pretty early, and I daresay you'll sleep in.'

'I know you'll have a great time, you

brave girl, and you'll come back a new person,' Jane assured her.

'Possibly a person broken into a thousand painful pieces, but we'll see,' Cleo laughed in reply, and gave her friend a quick squeeze.

She felt quite bouncy as she walked back to the ward. The hospital looked like a friendly place, with its regular rows of warm yellow lights, and darkness softening the somewhat severe outlines of its very functional buildings. She was glad she had made the change to Coronary Care, too. It was an interesting place to work, Sir Phineas Grimes appeared often enough to add an extra dash of spice, and—even Tony Fitzgerald wasn't too bad at times. They hadn't clashed over anything for nearly two weeks now. If this kept up, Cleo decided she might almost begin to like the man soon.

So she thought in her happy innocence and dreamy pre-holiday optimism, but she was destined for a rude awakening very soon. Dr Fitzgerald was waiting for her on the raised platform of the nursing station when she tripped lightly back into the ward, her cheeks pink from her brief contact with the crisp night air.

'You're late back.' He frowned and muffled a cough with his large fist. Cleo glanced at her watch.

'Two minutes,' she said defensively, the bubble of her happy mood pricked. And she had been ten minutes late going off in the first place.

'Two minutes matters on a ward like this,' the Registrar growled. 'You must realise that.'

'Yes...' muttered Cleo. Was it deliberate that he rubbed her up the wrong way so easily? He clearly disliked her as much as she disliked him. So much for her misguided decision to think better of him! It was very contrary of her, but the thought of his dislike piqued and annoyed her considerably. How dared he!

He was still looking at her from beneath lowered dark brows, and she felt suddenly dumpy and unattractive. Cigarette smoke from the dining-room clung to her hair and uniform, she was slightly out of breath after executing a number of excited skips and hops on her too-rapid walk back from dinner, and she was aware that she was still too plump.

'I wanted to give you some more instructions about Mr Edwards,' the Registrar was saying now. 'Perhaps we could go into the sluice room for a moment.'

'Oh—er—yes, of course.' Cleo was surprised, and showed it.

The suggestion was unusual. Was this to be a more serious reprimand about her work? She set her jaw knowing she had done nothing to earn one from him.

When Tony Fitzgerald had shut the door of the small room behind him, she faced him with her head held high—and was confused when he simply outlined the new drug therapy he had prescribed for Mr Edwards, and the special monitoring that was required for the patient's condition.

'You may need to call someone in the night. I'm only second on call, so it probably won't be me, but keep your eye on what you're doing, won't you?'

'Yes, doctor.'

'And by the way, I got your card,' he said heavily, taking Cleo completely by surprise with the almost casual words.

'My c-card?' she echoed.

'Your Valentine's Day card—several weeks late, of course,' he elaborated expressionlessly, pulling the thing from his pocket as he spoke and holding it out to her. 'I found it in my pigeonhole this afternoon. It seems to have got lost in the postal system somehow—perhaps because it's addressed so badly.'

Numbly, Cleo took the card from him and studied it. Her insides suddenly felt as if they had been snap-frozen, and she didn't need to wonder who had really sent it.

This accounted for several hints and

knowing smirks she had received from Shirley over the past few weeks. She had assumed that the other nurse was alluding only to the card Cleo herself had received, and she had been too excited about holiday preparations to be stung by the girl's manner, but this second card brought it all back again, and with an added edge of unpleasantness.

The card was of the humorous variety, and featured a pinkly naked couple with unlikely anatomies cavorting against a nondescript background. A nurse's cap had been added to the woman's head in black fine-point felt pen, and the man sported a jaunty stethoscope. Beneath the suggestive printed message inside the card, two more sentences had been penned: 'It worked for *Antony* and *Cleopatra*. I'll show you my Pyramids if you show me your Colosseum.'

It took Cleo only a moment to take all this in. The first sentence lacked the subtlety of a Shakespearean quote, but the second was a counterpart to what had been written on her own card. She felt quite sick, and when the card fell from her nerveless fingers, she made no attempt to pick it up.

Tony Fitzgerald did so, bending and retrieving it in one economical movement. Then he held it out to her at arm's length, lightly pinned between the tips of his finger and thumb, as if he found it distasteful to even touch the thing. He had flushed slightly, and Cleo knew that her own cheeks were pink. She stepped back.

'I don't want it.'

'And I damn well don't!' His low voice vibrated with anger.

'I didn't write it,' Cleo assured him intensely.

'No?' The quiet query contained a wealth of meaning.

It was too much for her. She stepped back again and lifted her head, meeting his very cool grey-blue eyes.

'You must have an *incredibly* low opinion of me,' she said fiercely.

'It's mutual, isn't it?' he replied at once, as if the fact that she disliked him didn't even begin to bother him. 'Some of your friends in the nurses' home probably know that, and this is their idea of a joke, although to my mind it's not very funny.'

His words, and the heavy tone, implied that Cleo shared the doubtful sense of humour of her nursing friends.

'What makes you think I even know who sent it?' she challenged unwisely, and gritted her teeth when he gave a sarcastic laugh in reply.

'It's written all over your face,' he said.

'If, as you say, it wasn't you, then you certainly know who it was.'

'What are you going to do about it?'

'Just this.' He tore the card into ragged quarters as he spoke and leant past her, aiming for a nearby bin.

'No!' Cleo held out an ice-cold hand and clamped it around his strong solid wrist.

'What?' He looked at her fingers coldly as if their very touch was repugnant to him, and she let go quickly, before stammering a reply.

'The bits aren't small enough. Someone might still...be able to read it,' she finished lamely. Was it likely that someone would bother to fish it out of a bin that contained hospital waste?

'Tear it up smaller then, if you like,' he said with heavy patience, then dropped the pieces into her hand and strode wearily out of the room and back on to the ward, rubbing strong fingers beneath his eyes as if trying to smooth away a thousand important cares.

Cleo scowled after his retreating figure—shoulders hunched, hands in his pockets now, and that hair rumpled as always. He had given the impression of being busy, but she noticed that he found time to stop beside Bed Two and exchange a few words with Angie Carruthers, who was on the same shift as herself for a change. The very attractive brunette seemed quite pleased that he had done so, what was more...

The incident stung terribly. And she knew that it was at least partly because of the warmth they had shared over Mrs Weldon and her Valentine cards. It seemed like a cruel irony of fate that their best moment and their worst moment together should be linked in such a way.

Would that have occurred to Tony too? Hardly likely. He had never mentioned the ninety-four cards to her, in spite of what Sam Weldon had said about the interest he had shown in them, which made it clear that he wasn't going out of his way to find common ground with her.

'It's just as well that I detest him too,' she said firmly to herself as she returned to her work.

By a quarter past eleven, Cleo was shamelessly counting the minutes until the end of the shift. She enjoyed her work very much, but it wasn't every day that she was about to take off on an adventurous holiday, and a week would scarcely be long enough to forget the nasty scene over that Valentine card. She had to be up again by seven in order to pack last-minute items and be on her way to the airport in good time. Roy Edwards' condition had remained stable after all, and there was time for several snatched minutes of daydreaming about the trip.

'Ouch! Sorry!'

Cleo's patient was in Bed Three, next to Angie Carruthers, and the dark-haired beauty had accidentally bumped some of Cleo's equipment. She was about to say that it didn't matter, when Katrina Foster, a third-year student whose patient occupied Bed Four, whispered anxiously across.

'Cleo, can you help me with something? I'm a bit worried. I don't know if I need to be, but...'

'Of course.' Cleo left her position and went across to the junior girl. At least half the nursing staff in the CCU were fully qualified, and no second or first-year students ever came here, but responsible third-years did, and were always placed next to a staff nurse or Sister, so that they could receive this kind of help easily. Nurse Foster's request was not an unusual one, therefore.

'See, I've just taken another BP reading and it's lower than the last one, which was lower than the one before that. What's wrong? That shouldn't happen, should it?'

'What medication is Mr Archer on?' asked Cleo.

'Xylocard.' Katrina pointed to the notation

112

of the drug and its dosage as she spoke.

'Well, then it's nothing to worry about. Falling blood pressure is one of the side-effects of that drug. He's only recently been put on it, hasn't he?'

'Yes.'

'Then it should level off soon. If it doesn't, we've cause to worry.'

'And anyway it won't be our problem, because we're going off in less than an hour,' Katrina returned flippantly and happily.

'I'm quite sure it's all right,' said Cleo. 'I was swotting up on drugs and side-effects just a few weeks ago.'

'I think I'll be an emotional wreck once I'm qualified—*if* I ever am,' the third-year sighed. 'The responsibility you lot have!'

'CCU is good training for that, actually,' Cleo told her. 'You'll be amazed at how much more you know and how secure you feel when you transfer to your next ward.'

She returned to her own patient, feeling a little smug, if the truth be told. Sometimes the feeling of being looked up to by juniors was rather a pleasing one...

On this occasion, the feeling was destined to disappear extremely rapidly, however. Cleo found it was time to take another reading of her patient's jugular-venous pressure. She did so, quite calmly, but when she read off the figure, her heart lurched in her chest. It shouldn't, it *couldn't* be that high! Was Mr Edwards' condition deteriorating in a major way and she hadn't even *noticed?*

Perhaps it was pre-holiday excitement, or perhaps a reaction to the smug confidence she had just been feeling, but whatever the reason, the fact was—Cleo panicked.

'Something's wrong,' she said urgently to Angie Carruthers. 'It's the j.v. pressure. I'm going to page someone straight away.'

'The senior houseman's up to his ears on A and E,' a tired switchboard operator told her. 'The second on call's asleep—I presume, since he's barely had a chance in the last three days. Shall I wake him up?'

'Yes!' said Cleo, realising too late that it was Tony Fitzgerald, and then deciding not to care. If a patient's life was in danger...

While she waited for Dr Fitzgerald to arrive, she made feverish checks on everything she could think of. Temperature, pulse, hourly rhythm strips—even though she'd done one at eleven. Nothing else seemed to be abnormal, and Mr Edwards had nothing to complain of—except the disturbance, of course.

When Tony Fitzgerald arrived, she hurried towards him, quite nervous by this time.

'Yes?' he growled briefly. His hair was more wayward than ever, his face was still creased with sleep, and there was a red mark on his cheek where he must have been pressing it against the edge of the pillow. Strangely, this disarray suited him, as did his casual grey pants and open white coat. The pale striped shirt beneath was buttoned, but only just. Cleo glimpsed a strong smooth chest, but wasn't really concentrating on details of that sort.

'The jugular-venous pressure—Mr Edwards —it's far too high,' she gabbled.

'Let's have a look.' He strode over to Bed Two, smiled at the sick man, and took a reading. 'That's ridiculous.'

Cleo hovered anxiously behind him. Roy Edwards' eyes had closed again, and she guessed he was really too sick to know what was going on.

'I know—I can't understand what—' she began, but stopped as Tony leaned forward to examine the equipment, then wheeled around to face her.

'The jugular line is blocked,' he said heavily, his provincial accent suddenly stronger from tiredness and anger.

'Blocked?' she could only echo squeakily, her heart beating unevenly.

'Kinked,' he elaborated. 'Look.'

And there it was. A very obvious kink too, which Cleo could not now

115

understand how she came to miss. She watched numbly as the Registrar twitched the tubing straight again, took another reading to make sure, then stepped away from the patient's bedside. Mr Edwards was already dozing unevenly again.

'May I go back to bed now?' Tony Fitzgerald asked sarcastically.

'I suppose so, unless you want to finish my shift for me,' Cleo returned, coldly and very unwisely. It was not the kind of thing you said to a Registrar, even in the heat of the moment.

He fixed her with a belligerent glare for a second or two, arousing all her antagonism and embarrassment once more.

'I *didn't* send that card!' she whispered fiercely, aware that Angie was standing nearby.

'Look, I really don't care at the moment whether you did or not.' His face suddenly crumpled into tiredness and he clearly couldn't be bothered pursuing the issue any further. He turned and left the ward without another word, and Cleo didn't even feel like making a face after him.

What was the point? They detested each other and that was that. The new episode with the Valentine card had proved it, but proof hadn't really been necessary. She had known it anyway.

'Oh dear,' sighed Angie Carruthers, exaggerating her already well-rounded vowels. 'That was probably my fault. I must have kinked the wretched thing when I bumped the bed.'

'Well, why didn't you say so, instead of letting me take the blame for the whole thing?' Cleo flared suddenly. It was unjust, but she was tired, overexcited about tomorrow, and worst of all, absolutely dying for a cigarette. Angie's face set huffily and she turned back to her patient's charts.

'I've probably got two sworn enemies on the ward now,' Cleo thought wearily later that night, as she sat up in bed and smoked not one but two cigarettes.

CHAPTER FIVE

The skiing holiday was fabulous after that last dreary and disastrous shift on the Coronary Care Unit. Cleo enjoyed every moment of it, from the bustle and jet-set feeling of the airport to the camaraderie of enjoying après-ski drinks with new acquaintances in the hotel bar at night.

As for the skiing itself...she couldn't actually claim to be swooping down the runs like a graceful bird, and her tortured muscles felt more like perished elastic than anything else, but at least by the end of the week she could get to the bottom of most of the slopes and feel exhilarated by the descent at the same time. And wasn't that the important thing?

Most of the other members of the tour party had been pleasant and good fun. Only one had been the type she loathed—a boorish young man whose chief aim in life seemed to be to drink the most possible alcohol in the least possible time. There had been quite a few smokers, of course, and while during the day she didn't have time to even think about cigarettes, at night she often had to say, 'No, thank you,' when they were offered around, which continued to be difficult.

The hotel food was good quality Nouvelle Cuisine, without rich, fattening sauces, and although Cleo was hungry after her long strenuous day on the slopes and tucked quite a bit of it away, she knew she was still losing weight and firming up all over.

As for the mountain air—after the murk of London, it was unbelievably fresh and crisp. They were lucky with the weather too. Now that it was early March, the days were longer and the air warmer, and they had several days of brilliant sunshine which reflected strongly off the white slopes and gave Cleo a glowing golden tan, just faintly dappled with tiny freckles on her nose.

It was only on the day before they were due to leave that the weather turned. It wasn't particularly cold. In fact, it had rained during the morning, making the snow heavy and slow. Now, in the afternoon, the clouds had lifted a little, but a sluggish wind blew, gusting unpleasantly from time to time, and there was a flat, dull light which made the undulations of the terrain almost impossible to judge.

Many of Cleo's party had only skied for a short while after lunch, and she somehow seemed to have lost the small group who had remained out. She had had a minor fall which they had not seen, and after struggling to her feet, she found they had all disappeared.

'I could stop,' she said to herself. But it was her last day on skis, and it was only three o'clock—although she did feel quite tired. It seemed a pity just to go back to the hotel and fritter away the afternoon drinking coffee, though, and fighting off the temptation to visit the resort pâtisserie.

'I'll just do all my favourite runs once more,' she decided.

For a while all went well, but the heavy snow was tiring her legs more than she realised, and when she somehow got out of control on a short steep stretch, she just didn't know what to do. She careered off the machine-packed trail and into the even soupier snow at the sides. There was a patch of low, straggling pine-trees looming ahead after what looked like a relatively flat stretch...

Looked like, but wasn't. In the flat light, Cleo hadn't been able to see that it actually dipped sharply, and before she knew it, she was approaching one of the pine trees, her head exactly level with its lower horizontal branches.

After this, everything was a blur in her memory—the slow, twisting fall, the sharp thump against her head, the agonising pain in her right leg, and then the merciful release of a temporary black-out. She came to, too dazed to do anything more than call very feebly for help, but another skier must have seen the fall, as it seemed only a short time before rescue was at hand in the form of the ski patrol.

Cleo relaxed, her head still swimming crazily. She was probably going to die, but at least someone would know about it and would save her if there was any chance at all...

Of course she wasn't really anywhere near death, but she felt that death might be a blessed release two days later in the local hospital, some fourteen miles from Les Deux Aiguilles. She had suffered a spiral fracture of the right tibia, a strained medial ligament, and was slightly concussed as well.

The ski patrollers had manoeuvred her leg into an inflatable rubber splint for the journey down the mountain, but it had been a slow and painful one in the difficult conditions, and Cleo gave way to tears more than once. An ambulance trip to the hospital followed, and the leg was now safely in plaster.

Administrative procedures had been difficult—Cleo had the usual nurse's discomfort at being in the rôle of patient for a change, and the language barrier was a problem. It was fortunate that Skimmer's Tours automatically included an accident insurance policy in the price of the holiday. The tour leader had been wonderful, returning Cleo's equipment to the ski-hire, packing up her belongings, and having them sent promptly down to the hospital. Her fellow tour members had clubbed together and sent flowers and chocolates too.

But natural depression and shock had set in, and now, after two restless nights in the unfamiliar hospital bed, as well as bouts of headache and dizziness from concussion, Cleo was the picture of gloom indeed. Up to a week in here, they had said, to make sure that there were no complications following the severe bump on her head, and so that she could learn to manage the crutches properly because the journey back to England would be a strain.

A week would feel like forever. Cleo had spent the whole of Sunday in bed, still nursing concussion and hiding from reality in sleep as much as possible, but this morning, a sunny Monday, she had struggled into a blue hospital dressing gown and was now sitting in the small but bright lounge-room that was shared by ambulant patients from several male and female wards.

It wasn't that the place was unpleasant. In fact it was almost as nice as St Valentine's, Cleo decided generously, but with none of the other patients speaking much English, and no possibility of any visitors... She thought of her parents still thousands of miles away in Canada, knowing nothing about what had happened to their younger daughter, and tears sprang to her eyes for the third time already that day, blurring and dazzling her vision in the strong mountain sunlight.

For a moment she stared at the floor, not even trying to blink them away, but the sound of the swing door bumping awkwardly open and a distinctly English exclamation of annoyance made her look up suddenly. Someone new, and someone English, had arrived, and she couldn't see well enough through her tears to find out whether he looked nice or not. That it *was* a 'he' was the only thing she could be sure of for several more seconds until she had searched in her pocket for a handkerchief and at last wiped her eyes.

A tall, broad-shouldered figure stood in the doorway surveying the room and at the sight of him—dark hair, dark brows, blue-grey eyes—Cleo actually shrieked aloud. The sound turned the attention of everyone in the room, including the man who had just entered, towards her.

'Cleo Fitzpatrick, by all that's blessedly wonderful, what are *you* doing here!' Tony Fitzgerald exclaimed, and she suppressed a delighted laugh at the colourful oath.

In her sheer astonishment at the coincidence of his presence here, and her relief at having someone to talk to, she forgot that she didn't like him, forgot that she had a broken leg, and almost didn't notice that Tony himself was handicapped by a sling on his right arm and a plaster on his left wrist, that reached just beyond his knuckles.

He seemed to have forgotten his dislike of her too, and was coming eagerly towards her, his eyes a bright, twinkling smoky blue in the strong mountain sunlight, and his lips widened in a fresh grin.

Cleo was on her feet in a moment, and was actually taking a step towards him when suddenly a warning bell jangled in her mind—crutches! But it was too late. She was in a tangled heap on the floor, and the crutches she had belatedly remembered were lying there too, one beneath her and the other out of reach across the polished parquet.

'Steady on!' Tony covered the remaining distance between them, his progress slowed by a discernible limp. From her position on the floor, Cleo now saw that his ankle was bandaged too—evidently a sprain. 'I'll help you up.'

'How?' she queried wryly, with a speaking glance at his imprisoned arms.

'Good God! We are a sorry pair!' he exclaimed disgustedly, evidently having overlooked his own injuries for a few moments in his surprise at seeing her.

But he was at a loss for only a second, and before Cleo had thought of how she was going to get to her feet again, he had taken the matter in hand. In hand? Perhaps not an appropriate phrase on this occasion. With his sprained foot, he reached out towards the crutch that lay beyond her grasp and drew it towards her.

'If you can manage to roll off that other crutch,' he said. 'And if I bend over, you can probably use my shoulder as a support while you get up. Are you in pain?'

'A bit,' she nodded, wincing. She hoped she had not done any further damage to the leg during her fall. The medical staff would have to check it later on.

'You should still be able to get up.' He glanced about him. One of the mobile patients had gone to call a nurse, but everyone else in the room, looking on anxiously, was just as handicapped as himself.

Cleo found that he was right, and all went well until she leaned too soon on one crutch and it slipped from beneath her on the too-smooth polished floor. Somehow she managed to bump her chin on the other crutch, bit her tongue painfully, and uttered a cry that brought an instant response from Tony once again. Careless of his imprisoned arms, he succeeded in pressing them to her sides, supporting her and preventing the fall.

In the circumstances, it could only be an awkward position for both of them, and Cleo found she had no alternative but to press her face into his shirt-clad chest as she made a final struggle for balance. Tony was breathing heavily, she noticed, as she was herself.

She also noticed, in the brief moment before she could at last lift her head and say, 'I'm right now,' a mingled scent of maleness and musky after-shave that was far from unpleasant.

'Are you sure?' he was saying, in response to her words.

'Yes,' Cleo nodded.

She could tell that his teeth were clenched as he spoke and guessed that his effort to save her from a second fall had given considerable pain to his injured arms. She became aware of her own body too. There was no dangerous pain, and she was sure now that no further damage had been done to her leg, but her blue dressing-gown was twisted awkwardly, as was the lacy white nightdress beneath it, and she wished she had got dressed this morning. The nurse had given her permission to do so, but she had been too despondent to take advantage of it.

'Don't move, while I pick up that other wretched crutch,' Tony was saying. 'And then I think we'd both better sit down before they put us in straitjackets for our own protection!'

Cleo laughed and glanced about her, her gaze melting the amused and still slightly anxious regard of several pairs of French eyes, including those of a nurse and an orderly who had both just hurried in.

'*Çą va?*' came a general chorus of questioning voices.

'*Oui, ça va bien maintenant, merci,*' Tony replied at once in what sounded to Cleo's untutored ears like excellent French. She was surprised. Somehow the command of a foreign language wasn't something she thought he'd possess, though why she felt this was hard to say.

Curiosity and concern subsided at his words, and everyone went back to their books and newspapers and conversation.

'Sorry about that,' said Cleo as Tony handed her the crutch awkwardly with his plastered hand. 'I just...completely forgot that I had a broken leg when I saw you standing there. Did you get hurt during all those manoeuvres?'

Her nursing instincts were aroused, and she welcomed the fact, aware as she was that her face was very flushed, and *not* because of her recent exertions. It was the memory of that chest firm against her face and the faint fanning of his breath against her hair that made her cheeks hot. He commented on the fact, as she at last found the opportunity to straighten her clothing.

'I'm fine, but how about you? Your face is rather pink. Are you sure there's no damage done?'

'Quite sure, thanks.'

He seemed to accept the answer, and then at last they were both safely seated.

'And now,' he said, 'you never answered my question. What are you doing here?'

'I should have thought that was hideously obvious by now,' responded Cleo, glaring down at the plastered leg which a nurse had just helped her to raise and support on another chair, so that it stuck out straight in front of her. Miraculously, the plaster had not been disturbed at all during her fall.

'Yes, but I didn't mean that, I meant *here,* in France. You, of all people. I mean, ten days ago...' Tony's voice trailed off. Cleo looked at his suddenly frozen expression and remembered that their last meeting had been utterly disastrous, and that they were supposed to detest each other. These facts were clearly uppermost in Tony's mind now too.

There was an awkward silence and Cleo found that she could no longer meet his gaze. She thought of the beer she had split down his suit, of the Valentine's Day card, of Roy Edwards' kinked jugular line, and of every clash and niggle that had ever taken place between herself and Tony—and there were so many of them!

It was just Cleo's luck that of all St Valentine's many doctors, it should be this one who turned up, so unexpected and so unwanted!

Unwanted? Suddenly it seemed petty and stupid to carry the grievances of a working world that was hundreds of miles away, into this completely new environment. Why not try and forget all that, if she could, and if Tony would let her, and enjoy the companionship of a fellow-countryman and professional colleague?

She found the courage to look up at Tony and saw that his frozen expression had disappeared.

'Obviously you've been on a skiing holiday too,' he said, his cheerful tone only a trifle forced, and Cleo realised that this signalled his having reached the same decision as herself.

'Yes,' she replied brightly, daring to study his face and noting that its veiled wariness had now dropped away. He had been wondering what her response to his unworded offer of a truce would be. 'Skimmer's Tours. I booked it at that travel agent in the shopping complex near the hospital.'

'Yes, I guessed as much,' Tony nodded. 'They told me they always recommend Skimmer's Tours, and that they'd had quite a lot of enquiries from St Valentine's people.'

'Mine happened on my last day,' Cleo told him, a mournful note creeping into her tone as she gestured at her plaster again.

'And mine on my first, would you believe? Although I'd skied before.' His voice was even gloomier, and accompanied by a deep, terse sigh. He stared at the ground. There was a short silence that hinted at things not said, and then for some reason Cleo suddenly found the whole thing incredibly funny.

Her golden laugh broke out, and though she tried to stifle it, she could not. Oh dear! Tony would think she was laughing at him and everything would be back the way it had always been between them. He was still staring down morosely, but even as she observed him, his expression began to change, and in another moment he was laughing too.

'What *is* yours, exactly?' he asked, when they had both regained a measure of control.

'Spiral fracture of the tibia, strained medial ligament, query concussion. What about yours?'

'Fracture of the left wrist, as you can see, mild sprain, as you can see also. And a brachial plexis injury. My arm's completely numb. I'm in for observation till they decide whether the numbness is cause for concern.'

'Well, at least we picked different things,'

said Cleo, and they both laughed again.

'The French have always suspected the English were mad,' mused Tony. 'I think we're helping to prove it. Did someone ski into you?'

'No.' She made a face. '*I* skied into a tree, and off a precipice—well, a drop I didn't see was there, and through a bit patch of what felt like porridge.'

'I got my ski-pole caught in a tree, then came down on my wrist, and wedged my ski-boot in the root of another tree.'

'So the wrist break is the most serious thing?' queried Cleo, trying to think up what she knew about brachial plexis injuries. For some reason, even though she was in a hospital, the world of medicine seemed very distant and irrelevant at the moment.

'No, it's the numbness in the other arm,' frowned Tony, suddenly serious. 'There's a chance of nerve damage, and they won't be able to tell for some days, probably, so I'll just have to wait. It's hard. If any have been severed, it could affect my career.'

'Oh Tony, no!' The exclamation that broke from Cleo's lips surprised both of them. Was it the concern and sympathy she would have had for anyone in that position, or was there something more personal involved? Surely not!

But Tony only raised one eyebrow and

gave a crooked half-smile. He didn't want sympathy, which was understandable. Cleo ached to give it to him, which was not.

'Let's not dwell on it,' he said. 'Worrying won't help. I'll face it if I have to. Tell me more about your holiday—*before* your unfortunate relationship with the tree! Was the skiing good?'

That night as she lay in bed thinking back on the day, Cleo could scarcely believe that the man really was Tony Fitzgerald, bane of her life at St Valentine's. It was as if this small mountain hospital was an oasis existing in a world of its own, where anything that had happened before, or anything that might happen in the future, had no meaning.

The sun had continued to shine brightly throughout the day, and Cleo realised for the first time that the backdrop to the compact wood and stone building was one of sheer beauty. The hospital was situated on the outskirts of a small yet regionally important mountain town. At this time of year, being just below the snowline, it was a little drab and colourless, but in spring the grass would become a dazzling green carpet dotted with a dozen different alpine flowers.

The higher slopes did not need to wait for spring to clothe them. The snow did that—metres thick in parts, settled and blown into an endless variety of patterns and shapes, revealing dramatic rock formations and giving way to stands of pine lower down. During Cleo's first miserable day in the hospital it had snowed, and the trees which had not yet been reached by sun were still feathery white, their branches weighed down by the load.

A terrace opened off one of the hospital's businesslike corridors, and ambulant patients could take their morning and afternoon tea there if they wished. It was Tony who knew this, and Cleo was embarrassed. He knew so much more about the routine of the place, though he'd been here less time than she had. Unlike her, he hadn't wasted time and energy in being depressed. He had insisted that they take their morning tea out there, although she had been reluctant at first, and he had been right, it was magnificent.

Because the beauty of the place wasn't simply visual. The almost tangible clarity of the air, with its faint fragrance of pine, the delicious contrast in temperature between strong alpine sunshine and crisp blue shade, the inner peace that came from simply sitting and watching the slow, silent changes in the landscape—a tree dropping its load of snow, the porcelain blue shadows of the mountains moving across the dazzling whiteness... These things all added up to a splendour that was almost an ache in Cleo's awareness, and made her forget that her body still felt jarred, and her head woolly.

'Thanks, Tony,' she had said to him after they had sipped their morning tea in silence for a while.

'For what?' His questioning grin was as fresh and open as the landscape itself.

'For making me come out here.'

He just shrugged and said nothing, but a wry expression passed briefly over his features and she knew he was thinking, as she was, of how surprising it was that they should both be sitting here like this.

Perhaps it was because of this surprise that each of them felt that they did not talk about their lives and their personal histories at all that day. They were separated at lunch, as all patients were served main meals in their wards, but in the afternoon they forgathered in the patients' lounge again, and played cards and Scrabble and Monopoly, struggling and laughing over the unfamiliar French versions.

There was a physical struggle too, for Tony, with his incapacitated arms, and this was further cause for amusement as he attempted to manoeuvre cards and letters and dice. Cleo had to do much of it for him.

She thought of his earlier concern over the possibility of permanent nerve damage in his right arm. Every now and then she could see that it was worrying him again, but he made no mention of it, clearly not wanting to inflict his anxiety on her. It was a selflessness that could only command her respect.

The honours of victory in their games lay fairly evenly between them. Cleo won at Canasta, through a combination of skill and luck, Tony's score in Scrabble was phenomenal and some of his words downright suspect, and in Monopoly, each acquired such an even quantity of property and assets that they ended up buying out the bank and declaring the game a draw.

As a games partner, Cleo found Tony to be quick-witted, mischievous, cool, and teasing by turns, and she was amazed, when her attention was caught by a tumultuous salmon and orange sunset behind the deepening blues and purples of the mountains, to realise that the day was already over.

How could it have passed so quickly and been so pleasant? Her injuries had been almost forgotten, and she felt heaps better. And why now, as she lay in bed thinking back on it, did she feel such a peaceful languor stealing over her, instead of last night's restlessness and tension? Was it just that she was getting better?

Before she had managed to answer this question satisfactorily, however, Cleo was asleep.

CHAPTER SIX

'They're sending me home the day after tomorrow,' Cleo announced to Tony three days later.

It was afternoon-tea time, another day of brilliant sunshine and crisp clean air, and he was sitting on the terrace frowning and tapping a foot absently against the leg of a wooden table as Cleo approached. Her handling of the crutches was much more adept now that her body's general aches, pains and bruising were subsiding, and the medial ligament injury was also beginning to heal.

Nevertheless, there was a door to push open and two steps to descend, which slowed her progress and gave her plenty of time to observe her fellow-countryman before she arrived at his side.

His hair was bright in the sunlight, touched with copper, and his face was tanning quickly from its exposure to the strong ultra-violet rays that penetrated the air easily at this altitude. His frame was large but firmly muscled, and he should have been sitting lazily, looking relaxed, but he wasn't.

When Cleo made her announcement, he looked up abstractedly and she knew that his thoughts had been far away and he had not noticed her approach. It was not the first time she had caught him like this over the past three days. Was it just his arm that was worrying him? Or was there something more?

'Sorry? What was that?' He looked up at last.

'I said they're sending me home the day after tomorrow.' She repeated the words jubilantly, but the moment they were out she realised it was scarcely considerate to sound so pleased when Tony's future was still so uncertain.

There were signs of strain around his eyes and mouth, and Cleo remembered scattered phrases she had heard about him at St Valentine's: 'studies amazingly hard', 'overworked', 'exhausted', 'stressed', 'incredibly ambitious'. Yes, and there were times, like now, when it showed, in spite of the tan and the naturally competent and healthily-proportioned body.

But before she could apologise for her

tactless enthusiasm, his expression had changed and brightened.

'That's excellent news, Cleo.' It was one of the times when his provincial accent came out more strongly—surprisingly pleasant on the ear—and she could tell he was sincerely glad for her. 'Going straight back to England?'

'Yes. The Skimmer's bus is going to come here and collect me, and I'll catch the plane from Geneva with the rest of this week's tour party.'

'My tour party—or some of them,' Tony told her.

'Some of them?'

'Some of us were booked for two weeks,' he explained.

'And...any decision about you yet?' she ventured to ask.

'Not yet.' The brevity of the response told her it was a subject he'd rather avoid.

She felt dispirited for some reason at the news, and it wasn't just unselfish concern for him. Had she been hoping at the back of her mind that they would make the journey back to England together? It was unwise of her if she had, because something told her that the friendship they had established over the past few days could have no existence outside of this unique environment. It was like a fragile alpine flower—a vibrant, beautiful, brief life here in the mountains, then wilting and shrivelling at any attempt to transport it to other climes.

'Here comes the tea trolley. Do you want some?' Tony was saying.

'Oh, thanks, yes,' Cleo replied confusedly.

She caught his speculative glance, his blue-grey eyes fixed on her for a moment before sliding away to gaze at the scenery when they met her own uncertain look. Had he been able to guess what she was thinking? Her cheeks grew hot at the very idea. They had been very foolish thoughts, and stupidly sentimental.

This was the companionship of two people thrown together without choice in a foreign place at a difficult time in their lives, and agreeing in a civilised British way to ignore their differences. It was nothing more, and could never be anything more.

As if to underline this fact, Tony turned away from her completely while she helped herself to tea, still stumbling in her reply to the ward maid's questioning *'Au lait? Sucré?'* although she felt she ought to be used to the words by now.

There was a new patient in Female Orthopaedics. She had arrived yesterday, suffering from an uncomplicated fracture of the left tib and fib—as Cleo phrased it to herself, using a standard professional abbreviation—and would probably be going home again tomorrow. It was only the fact that she had been mildly concussed as well which had kept her in hospital at all. She had manoeuvred herself out on to the terrace for tea, as had two or three more of the French patients, but had ignored the group into which they had clustered, and had sat beside Tony instead.

'*Bonjour, monsieur.*' Her greeting was clear and bell-like, and she was beautiful in a classic French style—dark, chic, olive-skinned, petite and fine-boned.

'*Bonjour, mademoiselle.*' Tony returned the greeting in his excellent French, and they began a conversation of which Cleo frankly could not follow a word.

It was annoying. She had not particularly wanted to talk before, having come to enjoy the silences she and Tony had often shared over the past few days as they peacefully absorbed the beauties of the landscape, but now she found she did, and there was no one she could talk to.

Actually, it was surprising that Tony had spent so much time with her and so little with the other patients, since his French was so good. It had been very polite and pleasant of him to think of Cleo's isolation, and she could not blame him in the least if he now decided to get to know someone else at the hospital as well.

If that someone else was clearly very beautiful and charming—almost a damsel in distress with that heavy plaster weighing down her small frame, and that awkwardly tight skirt, and an underlying tension in her manner too—then that too was perfectly normal and understandable.

Of course Tony would rather talk to someone whose black eyes twinkled constantly, whose head tossed animatedly, and whose silvery laugh rang out often—too often?—in preference to, say, that grouchy Gallic businessman who sat by himself in a far corner.

The word 'jealous' could not possibly be at all appropriate in this case, but there was definitely something wrong. Cleo felt clumsy and unattractive and hopeless—a familiar set of feelings that had been blessedly absent over the past week and a half. She contrasted the French girl's small graceful body with her own and felt like an elephant, although her weight loss was still steady and her muscle tone likewise improved.

The girl wore a silky blouse topped by a fluffy full-sleeved angora cardigan in a shade of pink that complemented her dark hair and olive skin perfectly. Her dark wool skirt was shaped to set off her compact curves, and even the plaster that disfigured her leg seemed like just an amusing if inconvenient trifle.

Cleo wore blue jeans, nice fashionable and quite expensive jeans, but plain. She had unpicked the side seam of one leg to accommodate the plaster, and rolled up the fabric to keep it out of the way. She had thought of cutting off the jeans leg, but that involved permanent damage and the consequent loss of a perfectly good pair of trousers, so she had decided on the more practical solution of unpicking instead. It would be quite easy to sew them up again afterwards.

Now she wished she hadn't thought of this, as the loose material was definitely bunchy and unsightly. Was it worth changing into her skirt? But she had worn that yesterday, and anyway it wouldn't go with this lacy-patterned teal-blue pullover.

Oh, but she was being completely ridiculous! Her tea-cup was empty. Shadows were beginning to fall on the terrace. She would go inside and read that American detective story she had started this morning. When Cleo swung her way past Tony's seat, crutches thumping rhythmically on the stone-flagged terrace, he didn't even glance at her, and it didn't matter a bit!

She didn't see him again until late in the evening.

The hospital was quiet at this hour.

There were fewer staff members about, and of course all the truly ill patients were settled down for the night. Cleo felt far too well by this time to lie in bed. She knew she would have already been sent home if the journey had not been such a long one, if she had had a friend or relative to accompany her, or if there had been a greater demand for hospital beds.

The evening had passed pleasantly if slowly, the time mainly filled by reading, and now it was time for a shower, which was still quite an awkward procedure.

Cleo wondered why Tony hadn't put in an appearance in the patients' lounge. She suspected that his condition was actually disturbing him much more than he was letting on, and thought he had probably retired early to rest his arm. It had taken her a while to notice how careful he was being with it, as he never drew attention to the fact. Sometimes, though, there was a wary expression in his eyes as he moved it in its sling, which she had now learned to interpret correctly.

She enjoyed her shower. It was interesting how, when you stopped being greedy for food, your body discovered other sensual pleasures which were just as good. She was able to keep the plastered leg dry because the shower was of the European type—easier to direct to one part of the body—with its hand-held shower-rose shaped something like a telephone receiver, at the end of a long, supple-jointed metal hose.

There was no one else in the bathroom. Many of the patients needed blanket baths, of course, and many others chose to wash in the morning. So Cleo could simply give herself up to the exhilarating feeling of covering her body—or half of it, anyway—with hot drumming needles of water.

It was just as she was thinking it really was time to turn off the water when the door opened and someone bumped their way awkwardly in, apparently unaware of Cleo in her enclosed cubicle, although there were clouds of steam issuing from it to betray her presence by this time.

She turned off the water and was startled to hear the sound of abandoned sobs and incoherent words.

'Je vais me tuer. Je veux mourir. Oh, mon Dieu!'

As well, there was the clatter of an aluminium crutch falling to the floor, and she realised that the apparently distraught woman was Solange Lelouche, the petite, dark-haired beauty whom Tony had been talking to today at afternoon tea.

The girl was nearly hysterical, but her

entrance was so unexpected that for a minute Cleo could not think what she should do. Go on pretending she wasn't there? Try to help in some way? Dry herself, put on her nightdress, gather her things and slip quietly out? *Could* one slip quietly out on crutches?

She heard the sound of an object—metal or glass—being set down on the porcelain shelf above the hand-basin, then traps running and hands splashing. She guessed that Solange was trying to cool and soothe her reddened eyes. But then the sobs broke out again, and it seemed obvious now that the girl needed help, even if it was just comforting words.

In what language, though? Perhaps it would be best to go in search of a nurse. She began to dry herself and was about to reach for her nightdress when she heard a new set of sounds. There was the unscrewing of a metal cap from a glass bottle, and the gurgling of its contents, then a horrible desperate and frightened choking sound.

More quickly than she would have imagined possible, Cleo was out of the shower cubicle, wrapping her towel hastily round her and tucking it in at the top, not bothering about crutches, but simply hopping on her good leg and bumping on her plaster.

In another moment, what had happened was clear.

With a spine-chilling crash of glass, Solange dropped the brandy bottle she had been drinking from into the sink. It drained away and released its pungent vapours into the steamy atmosphere of the bathroom. The girl's face was panic-stricken and purple, and she was fighting vainly for breath.

In a flash of insight, Cleo realised that she must already have been half drunk and had somehow swallowed the cap of the bottle as she took a swig from it. The cap was now lodged in her throat, blocking her breathing entirely, and this could prove fatal in a matter of minutes unless something was done.

She knew what that something was. It was a process known as 'the Heimlich manoeuvre', named after its American inventor, and quite a recent development. It wasn't difficult or time-consuming, but the vital question remained—would it be possible for Cleo to perform it, handicapped as she was by her precarious balance on the plastered leg?

'Help, somebody, help me quickly! Help! Au secours! Socorro!' It didn't matter how it sounded or what language it was in, as long as somebody understood and came. And if nobody did, Cleo knew she had to

try to do something herself. 'Just stand up straight. Stand still, please!'

Oh, if only she knew it in French, or if this girl spoke some English!

But Solange was too panic-stricken to respond to anything but authority and force, which Cleo doubted that she could give, injured as she was. She tried to get into position for the Heimlich manoeuvre, standing behind Solange and bringing her arms round to the girl's abdomen, forcing a fist below her sternum ready for the sharp inward and upward thump of pressure that she hoped would create a force of air sufficient to expel the dangerous object.

Solange did not understand, however, and tried to fight herself free in her desperate search for anything that would help her to breathe.

'Listen—I'm a nurse, please! I know what I'm doing!' Cleo was almost crying now herself, aware that time was rapidly running out, and that this girl was dying before her very eyes. 'Please help! *Au secours!*' she called again, and this time, at last, there was a response.

'She's choking? You're trying the Heimlich manoeuvre?'

It was Tony Fitzgerald. He had barged through the swing door of the bathroom, setting it—swinging crazily and squeakily, and had taken in the situation at a glance.

Careless of his still-painful sprain, he was beside the struggling pair.

'I can't get her to understand that I'm trying to help,' Cleo said effortfully. She completely forgot that this afternoon she had been almost jealous of Tony and this girl talking together, and thought only about the saving of a life. 'She's been drinking. It's the cap of the bottle.'

'My God, and I can't do it with my arm! *Ecoutez...*' He fired off an explanation to Solange in rapid French, but the girl was too desperate for breath to take it in properly, although she had stopped her active struggle. Tony switched to English again. 'Cleo, brace yourself against the basin. I'll manage to keep her still from in front somehow. There's not much time left.'

Quickly she acted on his instructions, pressed her fist sharply into the girl's abdomen, and at last succeeded. Solange coughed and retched and the bottle cap dislodged itself.

Tony reached into her mouth with his plastered hand and brought out the cap with his free fingers. The distraught French girl was gasping lungfuls of air, the dangerous purple of her face already beginning to ebb away. She turned and clung to the basin, too shocked and relieved even to cry. Cleo held her shoulders, afraid that she might yet collapse through shock or dizziness.

'There's blood on this,' said Tony. 'Its edges are quite sharp. It will have cut her and she'll probably have a very sore throat for a good few days. There's a risk of infection too, but the medical staff will deal with that.'

'But I don't understand how she came to have the brandy in the first place,' Cleo said now, perplexed. 'Surely, in a hospital?'

'That's easy,' responded Tony. 'Lots of skiers carry a hip-flask or equivalent on the slopes. It was probably amongst her things when she came in, but no one noticed. Anyway, stop worrying about that. You saved her life, Cleo.'

'You did,' she retorted.

'We both did, then.' He grinned suddenly, and almost roguishly, now that the drama was over and the tension had dissipated.

Cleo was suddenly aware that she was very inadequately clad. She let go of Solange to adjust her towel, which had slipped a dangerous inch or two lower, but as she made the move it came fully untucked and slipped open, revealing the full smooth curves of her breasts and hips. Convulsively, she clutched at it and pulled it back up before it slipped any further.

Tony, dressed still in day clothes, had

turned quickly away, but she was flushing all the same, deeply aware of his strong-muscled body, and when the door burst open again and a French nurse came hurrying urgently in, it was a welcome distraction.

Cleo felt at first that Sister Broche's arrival on the scene was tardy to say the least, but then she realised that in fact it was probably not much more than a minute since her last call for help. Sister Broche was breathless and concerned as she took in the scene.

'What 'as 'appened 'ere?' she asked, turning to Tony, who gave the explanation in rapid, unhesitating French.

Solange had recovered enough to listen round-eyed, her earlier hysteria and alcoholic haze effectively doused by her narrow escape from choking to death.

Cleo realised that she was about to be fulsomely thanked, so she gathered up her bundle of clothes and sponge bag and made a quiet if slightly clumsy exit on her crutches, under cover of the questioning and explaining that was still going on.

Why didn't she want to stay? She wasn't quite sure, but knew it had something to do with Tony. There was an elemental closeness two people shared when they helped each other to save someone's life. It had happened to her at the hospital before, of course, but not so dramatically and starkly, and not with Tony Fitzgerald. She wasn't at all sure that he was the person she would have chosen to share such an experience with, and yet...

Those blue-grey eyes of his had looked at her with such satisfaction and triumph after they had won their battle together, asking her to share in what he was feeling. She had begun to respond to his look, forgetting everything else, then her wretched towel had got in the way—and the feelings *that* moment had aroused in her were even more disturbing!

Cleo had a nagging and strangely unsettling sense of incompletion as she folded herself inside the crisp white hospital sheets, and smiled quietly at the Night Sister who was doing a round of checks on several patients.

But that wasn't too hard to explain, was it? It was because she was still worried about Solange. She still didn't know what had upset the French girl so much in the first place. That *did* explain the feeling, didn't it?

Of course it did, and that was why, when Tony explained the whole story to her the next morning, Cleo told herself that her mind was now set completely at rest. Or if it was not, that was because the story itself was rather a sad one.

'She rang her boyfriend to tell him about the accident,' said Tony. 'He wasn't there and he didn't ring back. Of course Solange was upset, but she rang again twice more and each time the girl who answered—one of his flatmates, because apparently it's a shared place with about five of them—insisted she'd told him and that if he hadn't rung back, what more could she do? Solange concluded that Armand didn't really love her, got herself into a state, drank too much, as you saw, which never solves anything—*et voilà tout!*'

'I'll just make a guess at those last three words,' laughed Cleo, appreciating his accurate mimicry of the French girl's volatile manner. 'But yes, it doesn't sound promising, does it? Maybe he's run off with the girl at the other end of the phone?'

'Maybe. He certainly sounds a bit heartless, anyway. I'd rush to the four corners of the earth if my true love was in trouble and wanted me to come—as apparently Solange had asked Armand to do.'

'Your true love?' queried Cleo, allowing a teasing note of surprise into her tone. 'I didn't know you were such a romantic.'

'Oh, I'm a hard-core case, or I will be, when the right girl comes along,' Tony replied lightly. Mockingly too, perhaps? Cleo couldn't tell. 'Or should that be a soft-core case, in this instance?'

'Soft, I think,' was Cleo's answer in the same light vein.

Inwardly, though, she found herself wondering about Tony's 'right girl'. What would she be like? Dark and petite, probably, she decided, thinking of the attractive contrast he had made to Solange yesterday as they sat together on the terrace. Suddenly she thought of Angie Carruthers at St Valentine's, too. She was dark and petite. Perhaps Tony had his 'right girl' in mind already?

They would make a good pair, Cleo concluded sensibly. Ideal, even. And there was no reason at all why *that* idea should ruffle her spirits.

She and Tony were not sitting on the terrace today, as there had been a change in the weather overnight. It was growing colder, and feathery flakes of snow were falling here and lower down in the valley, although they had not started to settle on the dull-coloured ground yet.

When they did it would be a pretty sight, with the geometric planes of the houses softened by white mantles like thick icing on a Christmas cake, but for the moment, the aspect through the double-glazed windows was a little dull. Cleo felt closer to the depression of her first day in hospital than she had at any time since Tony's arrival on the scene, and put it down to this change in the weather.

The imminent return to London and the stale days of a late city winter was in the back of her mind too, reminding her of a whole set of problems, familiar and new, that were yet to be faced. How much extra time off work would she have to negotiate because of her leg? She had already arranged to have four weeks, but would that be enough? Would Jane have found a flat? Or would she have to spend her convalescence in her room at the nurses' home—a room whose very walls at this distance of time and space seemed to be impregnated with the doubts and frustrations that she had resolved to overcome and escape from this year.

'Worrying about tomorrow?' Tony queried gently, breaking into the reverie she had not realised she had fallen into.

'How did you know?' Cleo cast him a perplexed sidelong look.

He seemed more relaxed today, and she had caught sight of his hastily-hidden frowns less often. The strained look was disappearing from around his eyes, and the casual clothes he wore—pale grey pants and darker grid-patterned flannelette shirt, with sleeves rolled up to the elbow-accentuated his new calm.

She wondered about it as she idly followed a movement in the muscles of his black-haired forearm, and decided to ask him. He was tapping his plastered hand lightly and slowly on the arm of his chair, but it was rhythmic in time to some radio music that was playing, rather than being yesterday's gesture of pent-up frustration and uncertainty.

'It's natural,' he was saying in reply to her question. 'You don't know how easy the journey will be with that leg. You don't know quite what you'll do with yourself till you come out of plaster. Of course you're worried.'

'And you?' queried Cleo, leaning forward and cupping her chin in a graceful hand.

'Me?' he smiled suddenly and broadly. 'Cleo, I think it's going to be all right. I haven't said anything, but I'm getting more and more certain. The feeling in my arm is beginning to come back and the doctors were pretty confident this morning.'

'Tony, I'm so pleased!' She forgot her own worries in the relief she felt for him, and was rewarded by a sudden and quite disturbing locking of their gaze. There was a clarity and intensity to those blue-grey eyes of his...

She looked down, too confused about his new effect on her senses, but he was speaking again, forcing her to look up.

'To celebrate, I've planned a treat for us, if you'd like to.'

'A treat?'

'An outing. This afternoon. Nothing major, naturally enough, in view of our mutual incapacitations,' he grinned wryly.

'Incapacitations? Did you just make that up?'

''Fraid so.'

'I quite like it.'

'I thought we'd just go and have a coffee somewhere, soak up a bit of French village atmosphere,' he went on, then sat back and waited for her response.

It seemed quite natural to agree to the plan. There was no reason not to, and to refuse would have been pointless and rude, yet Cleo suddenly felt that she was drifting into deep waters. What was it about this place and the days they had spent here? Things were changing and growing between them so fast.

She tried to conjure back her vivid memories of the anger he had provoked in her and the humiliations she had endured at his hands at St Valentine's, but she could not. She tried to remember that in England, at work, in the atmosphere of the hospital, she had found him boorish, arrogant, tight-lipped, unjustly bad-tempered...but none of those words seemed to fit this man at all. It really seemed that she was thinking of two different people and two different worlds.

This bewilderment within her did not lessen on their outing together, either. In fact, it simply got worse.

Cleo had to wear her ski-pants as they were the only garment she possessed in her luggage warm enough for an outdoor excursion and able to fit over her plaster. But they were fashionably-shaped, and the blue and white Fair Isle ski pullover she teamed with them brought out the colour of her eyes and had her fairly well satisfied with her appearance.

Tony had ordered a taxi—a tiny Peugeot which arrived on the dot of three, amid a rattling of snow-chains now that the roads were well and truly blanketed by the new falls. The little vehicle's cheerful driver helped Cleo into the back seat with a compliment in heavily-accented English, praising her loose silky blonde hair, that brought a laugh to her lips and a blush to her cheeks, especially when Tony added something of his own in French which she could not understand.

The driver darted round to the boot and deposited her crutches there, then they were away, skidding through the streets of the small town with a carelessness that had Cleo speechless with terror, though she was determined not to show it.

Tony wasn't easy to fool, however. He noticed her clenched jaw and white knuckles and chuckled softly.

'Don't worry,' he said. 'The man knows what he's doing. He could probably drive through a ski slalom course in this car if he had to, without knocking over a single pole.'

Still, it was a relief when they jerked to a halt outside a small but cosily-lit brasserie in a narrow street. It had been recommended by one of the orthopaedic ward nurses. Before Cleo was out of the car, the driver had her crutches waiting, and he presented them to her with a gallant bow, to which she could only reply with a halting, *'Merci bien.'*

They drank strong creamy coffee, but Cleo shook her head at the offer of a luscious array of cakes. Tony looked so disappointed, though, that she had to accept his next suggestion, which was that they share a small plate of Italian-style shortbread biscuits, dusted liberally with icing sugar. Probably just as fattening as the cakes, Cleo decided after tasting one, but after all this was a special outing.

Afterwards she tried to think back on what they had talked about, but could not remember at all. She only knew that somehow it was very intimate and very comfortable, and when she met the gaze of his blue-grey eyes, she did not want to look away.

'You've got icing sugar on your cheek,' he told her, just after both of them had finished their coffees.

The tables were quite small, and it was no effort for him to lean forward and reach his plastered hand across to brush away the fine white dusting with a lazy forefinger. The gesture was a caress, and it sent a strange new kind of shiver through Cleo that left her weak and almost trembling.

Could Tony possibly be going to kiss her? And if so, what would her response be? She knew the answer to both questions, and it seemed inevitable that his firm evenly-shaped lips would meet her own, across the table. Unconsciously she leaned forward, as he was, and let her eyes drift shut...

The bell at the door of the brasserie jangled and two more people entered.

'Tony!' The familiar name was spoken with a heavy French accent, in a female voice that shattered the spell that had been cast between them.

Cleo's eyes snapped open and she drew back, to find that Tony was already looking across at the new arrivals. He had sat back in his chair and she had a sudden horrible rush of certainty that that phantom kiss had only ever been in her own imagination.

The girl who had entered was Solange Lelouche, and she was followed by a young man who had been holding the door open for her. Cleo was favoured with a brief greeting in French, then Solange launched into a rapid-fire flow of words to Tony, accompanied by much gesturing and a fervent embrace with the dark-haired Frenchman at her side.

After Tony had spoken briefly in reply, the couple moved to some bar-stools at the opposite end of the brasserie, but Cleo knew that, whatever the meaning of the recent moment between herself and Tony—a moment suspended in time, it now seemed, unreal, imagined—it was now irretrievably broken.

'Well, she's certainly a whirlwind of emotion,' said Tony cheerfully. Cleo laughed, but the sound had a hollow ring to her own ears. He made no comment, however, but went on, 'That, as I'm sure you've gathered, was the errant Armand. It seems he jumped into his car and drove straight down here as soon as he heard about her leg, but had engine trouble on the way. The flatmate was just being vague—or vicious. The two of them are starting the journey back this afternoon.'

He spoke flippantly, but Cleo shivered momentarily. Solange's voice had creaked painfully once or twice while she was speaking to Tony, and she had swallowed very carefully, Cleo noticed, so her throat was still giving her some trouble.

'How awful if we hadn't been in time,' she said. 'Such a horrible accident, and all because of a meaningless misunderstanding.'

'I know.' Tony was sober now too.

The bell at the door jangled again just then, and again Tony looked up and smiled in recognition. It was the taxi driver, stumping snow off his boots before he came further into the brasserie.

'Surely that can't mean it's a quarter past?' Tony frowned. 'We haven't been here an hour!'

But it was, and they had. Cleo was surprised too, and the distortion in her perception of time seemed like yet another trick in this strange, unreal slice of her life. She slept restlessly that night, and had strange dreams, some with a nightmare quality, while others were hauntingly, achingly sweet. At three-thirty a.m., staring wakefully at the silent clock on the far wall of the ward, she decided it would be good when she was back and the hospital and things—feelings—were back to normal again.

It was still snowing the next morning at ten when the bus arrived, and the bad weather looked as if it might intend to stay for several days. Cleo was waiting for the bus, a little churned up in the stomach. She hadn't been able to eat much breakfast either. A hospital porter was ready with her things. and Tony was waiting to see her off too. He had just been for an examination and she could see he was jubilant. Managing to rise above her own not-fully-understood agitation, she asked him, 'How was it?'

'I'm a free man as of tomorrow,' he said, his wide, fresh grin breaking out as he spoke. 'No irreversible nerve damage.'

'Fabulous! And what are you going to do?' she asked, her heart lurching as she worded the question. How silly! What's happening to me? she chided herself inwardly before he replied.

'Don't know,' was his laconic response. 'Extend my holiday?'

They were standing in the snow at the back of the bus, watching her luggage being stowed. The hospital porter had departed, and Cleo had already made her halting farewells to those patients and staff with whom she now had a slight acquaintance.

The bus driver slammed down the luggage hatch and cast a grumpy and speculative look at the leaden sky from which thick flakes of snow still swirled in an apparently endless supply.

'I 'ave to mek a telefon call,' he said in

heavily-accented English, and stumped off into the hospital building, hands thrust into capacious pockets and shoulders hunched against the weather.

'What about your friends? They're not on the bus?' Cleo asked Tony, making conversation. For some reason the silence between them was awkward now, though all the silences they had shared during the week had not been.

'No,' answered Tony. 'I'm disappointed. There was a second bus, and they got put on that, apparently. Some are still up at Les Deux Aiguilles, staying on for the second week, of course.'

'It's a pity you didn't get to see them.'

The cold was biting into her gloveless fingers, and snowflakes were beginning to melt against the collar of her Wedgwood blue anorak and frost the edge of her wool cloche hat. It would be sensible to say her goodbye to him now and move inside the bus, but for some reason they both kept standing there.

'The driver'll be back in a minute,' said Tony, à propos nothing, and looking about him. He tried to rumple his hatless, snow-feathered hair with his left hand, in the gesture that Cleo suddenly remembered so well from St Valentine's, but the plaster got in the way.

'Well...' she began.

'Yes... Goodbye, Cleo.'

She started to look up at him, her lips parted to say the words back to him, but before she could do so, he had bent towards her and his lips had found hers.

They were cold and tasted of snow, but it didn't matter. Cleo returned the kiss, uncertainly at first, then responding to his gently exploring mouth. Almost at once she was no longer cold, but was filled with a fiery warmth that threatened to overpower her and drain her strength entirely.

She wanted to hold him, but knew that her balance was precarious in the slippery conditions underfoot, and that if she let go of the crutches she would fall. His left hand threaded around her shoulders then, as if he had felt her need for greater contact, and he drew her close and supported her in still greater warmth, as the snow fell upon them almost like a benediction.

His plastered wrist was hard against her shoulder blade, but she was barely aware of it, captured by the timeless moment, and by the melting strength of the sensations his lips were arousing within her. She could feel her breasts pressing into his chest and could tell that his breathing had quickened, as had her own.

'Cleo...' The name was spoken as a

caress against her lips.

She closed her eyes, forgetting everything but this, and it seemed as though their kiss might go on for ever, and she might stay warm for ever in his arms without wanting anything else...

'*Nom de Dieu, nom de Dieu!*' The bus driver's grumpy voice cut like a whiplash across their exploration of each other.

Tony released her and she opened her eyes, reality flooding in again. The bus rocked as the driver stumped up the steps and it seemed very possible that he might decide to leave her behind if she was not in her place quickly. She wanted to say something, but what? Nothing would come at all, not even goodbye, and Tony was silent too as he steadied her in the slushy snow of the roadway and held out his plastered hand for her to lean on as she negotiated the steps of the bus.

Before she could turn to face him again, to try to read something about what he was feeling from the expression in his eyes, the doors of the bus had wheezed shut, with a press of the driver's lever, and he was helping her along to her seat almost roughly.

'We meess ze plane, *mademoiselle*,' he said. 'Pleez, queekly!'

And before she knew it, Cleo was plumped down in her aisle seat, crutches stored above and leg stuck awkwardly out in front. She smiled uncertainly at the woman beside her and turned quickly towards the wind for a last glimpse of Tony as the bus ground into first gear and began to pull slowly away.

Yes, she could see that he was still standing there, a splash of colour in a red anorak, but his form was just a blur through the misted window and his features not discernible at all. She was leaving this place—a whole world of its own, it seemed—without knowing at all what that kiss had meant to him, and without any way of finding out.

CHAPTER SEVEN

London. Bleak, grey and windy.

As the French driver had predicted, the tour party had indeed missed their scheduled flight, more due to the snowy conditions and consequent treacherous roads than to the delay caused by picking up Cleo. They had been lucky to get a booking on another plane four hours later, and it meant arriving at Heathrow quite late at night.

Cleo ached with weariness. With her

166

plastered leg, the journey had been unusually tiring, and even though several fellow passengers had been friendly and helpful right up until their passage through Customs, they had then been claimed by friends and she had been left forgotten and feeling very alone. The large, echoing spaces of the airport building, the sleepless glare of fluorescent lights and the noise of planes jangled her nerves.

Foolishly, she had told no one she was coming back that day. The hospital's staffing department knew of her injury, of course, and that she would be off work for several more weeks. She had sent postcards to Jane and two other friends too, earlier in the week, but she hadn't known at that stage when she would be allowed to come home.

Now, of course, she was cursing herself for not ringing someone last night and asking them to come and meet her, but then... Then. Two different worlds. What—or who—had been filling her thoughts twenty-four hours ago, when she could have been planning for this lonely moment?

Tony Fitzgerald. And what was he doing now, hundreds of miles away in the French Alps?

With a cold sinking of her heart, Cleo realised that this morning's kiss had already receded in her mind, and her senses were blunted to the power of the memory. At first, in the bus, it had washed over her again and again, and she could almost feel his lips on hers, his plastered arm cradling her, and the warm rhythm of his breathing and pulses.

But now, tiredness and distance had intervened and the memory seemed more like a trick of the imagination. By tomorrow, what would she feel? She had, at the moment, absolutely no idea.

Careless of the expense, she took a taxi all the way from the airport to the hospital, and the driver, taking pity on her, carried her luggage up two flights of stairs to her narrow room in the nurses' home. Half an hour later, she had hidden from tiredness and misery in sleep.

There was a continual series of surprised exclamations when Cleo appeared at breakfast the next morning, handling her crutches quite expertly now.

'You're back, Cleo! When?' was Mandy's greeting as she adjusted her cap ready for a day on Paediatrics Ward Two.

'Last night, quite late,' Cleo told the plump, pleasant-faced staff nurse, who had been a friend since early in their training.

'I thought you'd go straight to your parents' place and stay there for a while.'

'They're still in Canada. They're due back in a week or so,' explained Cleo, tucking into a bowl of porridge. Life seemed only a little rosier this morning, but at least she was hungry, after waking quite early.

'Then who met you? Jane, I suppose, but...'

'No one met me.' Cleo broke in on her friend's trail of speculation. 'I got a taxi.'

'But you silly girl! I've got a car—lots of people have. Did you tell anyone you were arriving last night?'

'No, no one,' was Cleo's meek response to this tirade.

'Why on earth?'

'Oh...it was very late. Er—I'm not sure really.' The words came out lamely, but how could she explain the truth?

How could she say that she simply hadn't thought as far ahead as her arrival back at St Valentine's? And that for a time nothing had seemed real except that other hospital in the mountains, its sunny lounge and clean-aired terrace, and the presence of Tony Fitzgerald.

What was she going to say about all that? Some girls gave blow-by-blow descriptions of their romantic attachments—whether light or serious—to giggling groups of nurses in the coffee-room, some confided in a close friend, others chatted openly about a dozen boyfriends, and then suddenly announced their engagement to someone they had never mentioned before.

What would Cleo choose to do? It scarcely took a moment to decide. For far too many reasons, there was only one possible option. She wouldn't mention Tony Fitzgerald's name at all. What was there to say that was truthful, after all? 'I don't detest him any more.' 'We got on quite well.' 'He had a brachial plexis injury and a broken wrist.' 'He kissed me.'

No, above all not that, because that would demand a further explanation, and she didn't have one to give.

Mandy was hurrying to get her breakfast tray, and Cleo's other friends and acquaintances had already gone, so she was left momentarily alone at one of the larger dining-hall tables. For a time she forgot the coffee steaming at her elbow and the piece of toast growing cold on her plate and simply looked around her, her observation of this very familiar place sharpened by her two weeks of absence from it, and all that had happened during that time.

You couldn't call it an attractive place, especially not now, at breakfast, its plainest and most functional meal. Nearly everyone was a little creased and bleary-eyed, either from recent sleep or from a long night on duty. Small groups of housemen came and went, pairs of nurses, and a lone figure here and there who was in no mood for conversation.

Everyone seemed oblivious to the pale green walls, the constant drumming of jets of water in the metal sinks in the kitchen, the chink of cutlery, and the practical layout of trays and plates, tables and serving hatches.

As Cleo stared about her, Shirley Byrne went past in uniform on her way to her ward. They exchanged a cool, insincere smile, and suddenly all the events that had seemed so unreal and unimportant last week in France came flooding back. Without thinking, Cleo reached into her bag, her hand searching unconsciously for a little rectangular box of thin cardboard. It was only when her fingers could not find what they were looking for that she focused her mind on the action and realised what she had been doing.

Cigarettes! Had she thought of smoking even once after Tony Fitzgerald's arrival last week? No! From the kitchen came the crashing rattle of a load of crockery being slid roughly into the industrial dishwasher, and behind her, laughter from a group of orderlies. She was definitely home again!

'I'm really going to have to gulp this lot,' it was Mandy, returning with her tray, 'or I'll be frightfully late.'

'I don't suppose you know Jane's roster

this week?' asked Cleo.

Mandy was a good friend, but not as close as Jane, and she felt the need of a close friend at the moment. As well, she was trying to be practical, and realised that with a lot of free time stretching ahead of her, she'd be able to concentrate on flat-hunting, so she and Jane needed to get together to discuss future strategy and almost certainly modify their requirements. There was no point in dwelling on the past, especially when she was so confused about it.

'Oh, she's off till Wednesday,' said Mandy. 'She got her roster changed so she could get settled... Cleo! You probably don't even know yet!'

'Know what?'

'She's found you the most fabulous flat you could possibly imagine!'

'Careful! We don't want to bump the woodwork.' Jane hovered about like an anxious bird as Mandy and Gail manoeuvred Cleo's desk in the spacious bedroom that was to be hers for the next three years if all went well.

Cleo, encumbered by plaster and crutches, and sitting on a comfortable, good-quality couch, felt a little guilty that she was getting out of all this hard work. Fortunately, though, the flat had been almost completely furnished already, so apart from personal belongings, the work-desk was the only heavy item she was bringing in.

After making her startling announcement, Mandy had rushed off, saying she was already late and that anyway Jane would want to tell the story. She had just found time to scribble the address on a scrap of paper, and after breakfast Cleo had hunted it up in a street directory, plotted a route and taken the short bus journey there.

Earlier in the morning the weather had been dull, but as she arrived at the address she had been given the clouds started to break up, and a strong shaft of early spring sunshine beamed on to what looked like an impossibly magnificent detached two-storey stone house, dating from Victorian times and surrounded by quite a reasonable-sized garden.

Flat Three. Cleo found the ground-floor entrance and rapped sceptically on a glass pane, not expecting it to actually be Jane who answered. But it was, and she pounced eagerly on her injured friend and dragged her in for an excited tour of the high-ceilinged yet cosy two-bedroom arrangement.

'Isn't it fabulous?' she beamed.

'So fabulous that I can't see how we can *possibly* afford it,' Cleo frowned, bewildered and privately convinced that Jane had gone quite mad.

'Well, you see, as ever it's a case of "not *what* you know, but *who* you know",' Jane replied airily.

What had happened, it seemed, was this: Jane's Aunt Louise had been singing her praises as a flat-sitter to a diplomat friend who was due to go overseas for a three-year posting, and the friend had offered the flat to the two girls at a much-reduced rent, in return for the security of being able to leave most of her possessions—and her cat!—behind, knowing that they were in safe, responsible hands.

'Talk about fairy godmothers!' Jane had finished up, and so now, the very next afternoon, Cleo was moving in.

'What's to do after this?' Gail asked briskly, taking off her glasses to polish away some dust.

'Two more boxes, I think, not heavy ones,' answered Cleo, 'And then that's it. I'll make coffee, shall I? I feel so lazy and useless.'

'Rubbish! This is fun.'

The girls were already going back to Mandy's car in search of the boxes, so Cleo got to her feet and swung her way into the airy tiled kitchen. There was no instant coffee, but Claudia Hoffman, the diplomat friend, had left quite a few staple foods, including a packet of ground coffee, and said it was all to be used.

It was wonderfully satisfying to be making coffee for friends in her own kitchen, Cleo thought, as she moved about. She had spent last night in the nurses' home and had hated every second of if, not because the place was really so bad—after all, she had lived there happily enough for four years—but because it had somehow become associated so strongly with unpleasant memories of the first two months of this year: her struggle to give up smoking and lose weight, Shirley Byrne's malicious and distorted sense of humour, and her antagonistic relationship with Tony Fitzgerald.

It seemed so important not to take a step back into that time, yet the atmosphere of the place was already closing over her head like water, and she felt that she would drown in it and be sucked down if she did not get away.

Over dinner last night, Shirley had slid into a seat at Cleo's side and asked her a falsely sympathetic question about her leg, following it up with, 'I heard Dr Fitzgerald had gone on a skiing holiday in France. I don't suppose you saw him?'

'The French Alps *are* quite large,' Cleo had replied, avoiding a direct answer.

But what was Tony doing now? she

wondered as she made the coffee. She would hear from him soon, wouldn't she? 'Extend my holiday,' he had said in answer to her question about his plans. How long for, though? Perhaps he'd be back at the hospital in a week. Or was it completely stupid to look forward to seeing him? The phrase 'holiday romance' floated into her mind. She knew it was the kind of thing a lot of people did—a pair utterly unsuited to one another engaged in some light flirtation or affair that could not possibly have happened in their day-to-day environment. Physical attractions inflated artificially when there were no other distractions.

Was that all it had been? Lying awake last night in her narrow bed at the nurses' home, Cleo had been quite convinced that it was. Today, in the bright blue and white tiled kitchen, she struggled to believe something different. It had been real for *her*.

Or had it? Already it seemed impossibly far away. And how could something be real when it followed so closely on just as real a feeling of dislike and antagonism? The confusion and doubt nagged at the back of her mind and threatened to spoil this exciting afternoon.

Cleo turned her attention determinedly back to the coffee. The water had boiled now. She had the coffee grounds and the cups, milk and sugar, but what was there to brew it in? A quick look at the broad expanse of grainy wooden bench top revealed a Pyrex jug and plunger.

Actually, it was exactly the same as the one reserved 'For Sir P.' on Coronary Care, even down to the colour of the plastic components—dark blue. The only difference was that this one was larger.

Sir Phineas Grimes. Again Cleo felt a sense of dislocation and doubt. She had not thought about the distinguished cardio-thoracic consultant once for over a week, and yet before that he had figured almost daily in the daydreams that floated amongst her thoughts. Suddenly an image of him flashed before her mind's eye, triggered by what she was doing with the Pyrex jug.

'Thank you, Nurse,' the caressing velvety politeness of that deep voice when she handed him his coffee, his dark eyes and smooth, full lips bestowing the faintest of rewarding smiles upon her, then later, the immaculately fashionable tailored shape of his silhouette as he walked confidently and almost sinuously from the ward.

Two and a half weeks ago those things had thrilled her utterly. Now, there was no lurch of her heart, no tingle in her spine when she thought of him at all. Oh, what on earth was happening?

'Refreshments served for the hungry workers?' Jane popped her lively head around the door.

'Just about.'

'We'll loll in the lounge, shall we?'

'What if we spill something?'

'We're nurses. We're careful,' Jane assured her flippantly.

'Some of us have been known to have nasty accidents,' Cleo retorted, pointing down at her plaster. But then they agreed that they couldn't afford to be too nervous about their new home.

'...Or we won't get any pleasure out of the luxury at all, and we might as well be living in a grotty mud-coloured place where you can pour whole cups of tea into the carpet and no one even notices,' Jane concluded.

'And if the worst comes to the worst, and we do ruin something,' Cleo added, 'we'll simply have to pay for it or replace it.'

The general consensus, as they sipped their coffees and crunched on some savoury biscuits, was that Jane and Cleo were absolutely unfairly lucky, and there was bound to be a catch somewhere.

'But there's even a cat!' groaned Gail, as a dainty-pawed black-and-white pussy made her appearance, via a special cat-door built into the back door that opened off the kitchen. 'I'd *adore* a cat!'

'It means scraping out blobs of nasty smelly cat-food on to her plate twice a day, though, think of that,' said Jane, trying to sound as though this was the most horrible hardship possible, but not really succeeding.

She and Cleo exchanged a smile of satisfaction, and the latter felt that life was just too much at times. If there was something, other than the simple passing of time, which could make her disturbing and confusing feelings about Tony Fitzgerald subside, it was living in this gorgeous new place.

CHAPTER EIGHT

'Nothing for you today? Bad luck!' said Shirley Byrne with faintly mocking sympathy to Cleo. She stood, leaning one sharp-elbowed arm against the edge of the wooden pigeonholes where staff mail was alphabetically placed, watching Cleo leaf fruitlessly through the tidy pile in the 'F' pigeonhole.

A cigarette dangled casually from her

fingertips, and she blew a waft of smoke in Cleo's direction, as if she knew that the latter's craving for nicotine had not yet completely subsided.

'Doesn't look like it, does it?' Cleo replied brightly to Shirley's question. 'But are you waiting to get to the Bs? Reach above me, I don't mind.'

'No, I've got mine already, actually,' Shirley said. 'I'm just curious as to why you're getting letters delivered to the hospital. I thought you'd have given everyone your new address by now.'

'Well, some people haven't caught up yet,' said Cleo, biting back a retort that it was none of Shirley's business, and forcing herself to speak smoothly and naturally.

She had a horrible and probably unjustified feeling that Shirley knew who she was hoping for a letter from. There was a keen glint in the sharp-faced girl's round, innocently-widened eyes that gave the disturbing impression that some kind of game was being played here—a game Cleo did not understand.

'Yes, I suppose you might have friends abroad, or who've moved themselves, and you can't get in touch with them,' nodded Shirley calmly, then she turned and left, a faint smile playing about her pale pink lips as she paused to drop her cigarette end into a nearby bin.

Cleo waited till the other girl was out of sight, then leaned her forehead against the cool wooden panelling next to the pigeonholes, and let out the breath she had been holding in a deep sigh. Shirley's last comment had contained uncomfortable echoes of the truth. Her hands were almost shaking, and in an effort to still them, she clutched more tightly at the bundle of F letters she was still holding. In it, there had been two letters—both unimportant printed circulars—for 'Dr A. J. Fitzgerald', and she had flinched as she registered the name both times.

It was now a Friday in mid-May. Two months since her return from France, and in that time she had not received a line from Tony. It had become a ritual for her to call at this spot each weekday to check the letters, even though, until her recent return to work, it had meant a special trip to the hospital.

At first there had been quite a stream—a final card from her parents before their return, a letter from her sister Nancy, nursing journals, bank statements, other odds and ends. But now that she had let more and more people know of her new address, the stream had dwindled to a trickle, and she knew she would not be able to justify this daily leafing through the pile for much longer, even to herself, let alone to others.

It was not that she was *so* surprised that he hadn't written. She had, after all, told herself again and again that that interlude in France had meant nothing to either of them. One kiss, a brief shared loneliness and need that had blinded them both to the reality of each other, a holiday romance—or not even that; a tiny flirtation.

After two weeks, in her realistic moments, she had stopped expecting to see a postcard or a thin air-letter addressed to her in the scrawling handwriting she knew from his medical notes, and had started to look for the man himself instead—suddenly rounding a corner in some passageway, or striding across the hospital carpark, his sprain healed, his right arm fully mobile and capable, and rumpling his hair again in the familiar gesture.

But there had been no sign of him, and it was more for this reason, she told herself, that she flipped so religiously through the Fs. She wanted to find out if he was still employed at St Valentine's at all. Did personal letters still come for him? Or just printed ones like today, which might suggest that he had moved elsewhere and told all his friends of the change. Every now and then there *were* personal letters, but the next day they were always gone again, and Cleo guessed that someone was collecting them for him and sending them on. But to where?

She straightened up from her position against the cool, supportive panelling. Her thoughts had taken this dead end route hundreds of times now. Rubber-soled shoes echoed in a confident male stride out of sight around a corner in the corridor, and in the seconds before the man appeared, Cleo again felt the crazy stumble in her heartbeat, and the sudden wave of prickling heat that washed over her. Tony...?

A tall man, whom she dimly recognised as a member of the administrative staff, rounded the corner and crossed on out the door.

Suddenly she felt a hot spurt of anger against the Registrar from Coronary Care. He would have sent a postcard, if only to signal clearly to her that the timeless interlude in France had meant nothing to him:

'Just dropping you a quick line to say that I'm enjoying my extended holiday, and am well on the way to being fit again. I've decided not to return to St Valentine's, so I probably won't see you again, but I'll be eternally grateful for the way you brightened a fellow-countryman's lonely days in his hour of need! Thanks, Tony.'

Something very flippant and very final like that, so that she could put the episode behind her once and for all. Yet he had not cared enough to do even that.

Yes, she *was* angry, yet quite impotently, because it was becoming almost certain now that she'd never see him, never have a chance to vent the anger either in hot words, or in cutting and frosty disdain.

It was terrible that this gradually-unfolding realisation should have happened, because it had been a lurking shadow beneath what would otherwise have been very pleasant days, Cleo thought, as she finally left the hospital building and began the moderate walk home.

She was still exhilarated by the simple fact of being able to walk normally again, and though her leg was still weak, it was strengthening every day, and she was being careful to exercise it into fitness gradually, by walking and controlled stretching, and several physio sessions at the hospital.

The walk between St Valentine's and Flat Three, 36 Charlotte Lane was a delightful one at this time of year. It was an upmarket suburb, with large well-cared-for gardens that were bursting into spring life and colour. Number thirty-six's own garden was a riot of flowers and new growth, and during her convalescence Cleo had spent many an enjoyable hour working in the section of it that was Flat Three's responsibility.

The weeks before her return to work had passed largely in this kind of lazy pottering. She had spent two of them being mollycoddled by her mother down in Devon, where she had also renewed her acquaintance with childhood haunts, looked up old school friends and heard in detail about her parents' trip to Canada and the rigours of Nancy's lifestyle there.

Back at Charlotte Lane, she had arranged her room beautifully, growing to love the tasteful items that Claudia Hoffman had generously left behind, and augmenting them with precious old things of her own. Many hours had been spent in sewing, and many more in perusing recipe books and scouting around the shops in order to prepare a series of delicious yet crisply healthy and non-fattening meals for herself and Jane.

Cleo was now a trim yet gracefully-curved size twelve, her skin was clear, her hair lustrous and bouncy, and that instinctive craving for nicotine she had felt so strongly during her first breakfast back at St Valentine's recurred only sometimes. She had given in to it twice after fruitlessly looking for letters under F, and had hated herself for a while, but the desire was lessening, and she really felt now that she had beaten the addiction.

Her skin was even tanning a faint glowing gold now, from the hours she spent working in the garden, or simply sitting there with a book, and Lucinda purring sleepily on her lap.

If only the anger and hurt and confusion that nagged at her when she thought of Tony Fitzgerald would disappear, then a rich and full contentment might be hers!

Work was going well too, since her recent return, although there as well she thought far too often of Tony. It made her jumpy, because unconsciously she kept expecting to see him, and each time the door opened she flinched, confused as to what she would feel if it *did* turn out to be him one day. The old anger and dislike, intensified by the new reasons she now had to feel resentful of him? Or would there be a dropping away of all that and a return to the mood of that glowing, distant and unreal week in France?

None of the staff mentioned him on the ward, but of course they would have heard any news about his changed plans while she was away with her broken leg. The news would be stale now, so it was scarcely surprising that it was not spoken of.

There was another reason to feel on edge at work too, because of course Sir Phineas Grimes had come back into her life. On her very first day in Coronary Care she had made coffee for him, and had been thanked in the usual brilliant and blank way. Since then, however, he had actually favoured her with some brief chats, and Cleo realised that her new trim shape and sparkling hair and complexion had made a slight impression on one male, at least.

She was smiling to herself and thinking about this very thing as she walked along in the slanting sunshine of the late spring afternoon, when she became aware that a car was purring slowly along beside her. A quick sideways glance told her it was none other than Sir Phineas himself, and could it really be possible that he was slowing down because of her?

The proud-nosed cardio-thoracic consultant had indeed stopped his dark-green Bentley now, and was leaning across to the passenger side to wind down a window and speak to her. Cleo started to walk around to the driving side to save him the trouble, but he did not see, so she hesitated and then went back to the footpath again feeling awkward and flushing faintly at the thought that he was going to speak to her outside of the working environment at last.

For the first time since her return from France, Tony Fitzgerald seemed completely unimportant, and she was sure she was going to be able to do what *he* had so obviously done—dismiss those few days as the product of a unique set of circumstances, and never expect them to affect her life again.

'I'm afraid I don't know your name,' came Sir Phineas's low drawl. 'But I know you're a nurse who's recently started work on one of my wards, and we seem to be going in the same direction. Would you care for a lift?'

'Yes, please. I mean, that's very kind of you. And my name's Cleo Fitzpatrick.'

'Cleo! How unusual and lovely.'

He ignored the fact that her words had come out breathlessly, almost a stammer, and was opening the door for her—the catch gave way with a rich, smoothly-oiled click—and she climbed fumblingly into the spacious machine, attempting a smile which she hoped was a dazzling one.

Of course she hadn't 'recently' started work on Coronary Care, but the fact that he didn't connect her with the low specimen who had made coffee for him and listened respectfully to his instructions for two months over winter only paid tribute to the radical change in her appearance, so she didn't miss his mistake a bit.

'I take it you're visiting a relative out this way, are you?' he was asking languidly now, careless hands on gear-stick and steering-wheel as they glided forward at a moderate cruising speed.

'No, actually I live in Charlotte Lane,' Cleo explained, rattling the words out a little too quickly in her nervousness and sheer awe.

She stretched her legs out luxuriously. There was so much *room* in here! What a pity she was in her boring old uniform! Any woman at Sir Phineas's side ought to be wearing silks, furs and jewels...

'You live in Charlotte Lane?' was Sir Phineas's reply, astonishment breaking out above the normally laid-back tones of his deep voice. Cleo almost thought that over one vowel his impeccable public school accent had slipped too, but that must have been a trick of the car's acoustics. Then he added, sounding faintly annoyed, 'Oh, with your parents, perhaps.'

'No, actually in a flat belonging to a friend of my flatmate's godmother. You see, she's in the Diplomatic Corps, and she's been posted overseas—the friend, I mean, not the godmother, so we've got it at a reduced rent in return for—'

'Ah, I see, of course,' he broke in smoothly, and Cleo realised the explanation had been far too long and garbled. 'A rented flat. I was surprised because, you see, I live in Charlotte Lane myself, and know all the houses in that street to be quite

189

large and more than a little expensive.'

He laughed a well-modulated chuckle, and Cleo joined in more out of politeness and a desire to earn his approval than because she had really been amused. He seemed to have fairly rigid ideas about social caste. She knew several nurses who were very well off indeed, and several more who came from homes where poverty was a daily reality. Nursing was a profession that could take in all types, from all backgrounds, and that was one of the things she liked about it. Still, in the exalted circles in which he moved, one might easily acquire an inaccurate perspective of these things.

'So perhaps we're neighbours,' she ventured after a small silence.

'Hardly,' he retorted drily, reaching out to brush a finger lightly against her cheek in a tiny caress that took the sting out of his words but left Cleo almost gasping. 'I'm very well acquainted with all my neighbours. I'm at the far end of the street—Number 170, and I imagine you're probably much lower down.'

'Yes, just here, actually,' Cleo pointed hastily, recovering herself just enough to bring out the words in the nick of time.

He slid to a smooth stop right outside the house and so, far too soon, the short drive with him was over. Cleo began to say thank you, trying to pitch the words at the throaty purr that a companion of Sir Phineas Grimes should have, but it didn't work, sounding merely hoarse and unnatural.

Anyway, he didn't let her finish, but laid a detaining hand on her arm and smiled dazzlingly at her, his full lips parting to reveal very white and very even teeth. A ray of late sun glinted on his grey hair, turning it to spun silver. Cleo sat, frozen by the moment, scarcely able to listen to what he was saying.

'You're unusually attractive for a nurse,' he drawled. 'I wonder what you look like in something other than your uniform. May I be allowed a chance to find out? Will you dine with me tomorrow night?'

'Oh—yes! I mean, are you serious?' Cleo stammered.

'Of course I am, you odd young creature. Shall I pick you up at eight?'

'Eight. Yes, all right. It'll be lovely.' She opened the door and slid her legs out, pulling the edges of her navy cape together, and trying to make each of these movements smooth and graceful.

'You're blushing—how refreshing!' Sir Phineas imprisoned the hand that had been adjusting her cape and drew it towards him to plant the faintest of kisses there.

The gesture stunned rather than stirred

her, and when at last she was out of the car, standing on the kerb and watching him drive away, she found she was still holding her hand at eye level in front of her, as if it were no longer a part of her. She lowered it gently and went on watching the dark-green Bentley.

She saw the silhouetted figure in the driver's seat take a hand off the wheel to wave to someone further along the footpath, and then, seconds later, he had rounded a bend in the road and was lost to view.

Cleo began to walk slowly towards her front gate, idly watching the jogger who was coming towards her. He was the person to whom Sir Phineas had waved, and for that very reason, had a certain aura for her...

'Cleo?' The jogger suddenly wheeled to a halt and spoke her name.

She looked again more closely, and felt the strength drain rapidly from her limbs so that she might have fallen, had she not grasped one of the posts of the white picket fence that fronted the garden. It couldn't be Tony Fitzgerald—but it was!

'Hullo,' she said uncertainly. Politeness demanded it.

'Hullo, Cleo,' he replied, as if he found it difficult to use her name now, after his first unthinking greeting.

In the short silence that followed after this, she found time to decide that her failure to recognise him straight away was scarcely surprising. He looked tanned, fit, relaxed. His hair, together with his dark brows, had golden lights sunbleached into it. He wore navy and white shorts, socks and running shoes, and a sportsman's T-shirt—white too, and picked out in navy. The shirt's collar was open and the three studs below the neck undone. There was a faint mist of sweat around his collarbone, and his breathing was heavy after the exertion of his run. Cleo felt plain and clumsy in her uniform, in contrast to this perfectly-proportioned athletic-looking man.

'You're back,' she said. Scarcely the most scintillating comment in the world, but she was so uncertain about how to react to his sudden presence. Half an hour ago—only that!—at the hospital letter-rack, she had felt anger against him. Was that what she should be expressing now?

'Yes, I am,' was his reply, accompanied by a brief nod.

'You're looking well.'

'Italy suited me.'

'Italy...' Cleo nodded slowly.

'Yes, it's a fabulous country,' he enthused. His accent came through strongly, and she remembered how in France she had found it delicious on the ear. 'I hadn't been there before, and to tell the truth I was a bit lazy. I could have seen a lot more than I did. But what I did see! The churches, palazzos...!'

'So you had a generally wonderful time?'

She *was* feeling angry—or at least bitter—by this time, and didn't try to hide it. He was chatting cheerfully to her as if she were a casual acquaintance, and as if he had been away for two weeks, not two months. There was a slightly forced note in his tone, perhaps, but that only made her feel worse about him.

Tony had picked up on her frosty manner by this time. 'Yes, I did. I needed the holiday. You seem to find that unacceptable.'

His breathing had slowed already to its normal pace, and the words were delivered in a controlled deliberate way that sounded something like the Dr Fitzgerald she dimly remembered from Coronary Care but nothing like the man she had thought she was getting to know in France. He was looking at her steadily now, as if waiting for her to parry his challenging comment, and she searched for words that would do so. In the end she decided on a light response.

'Unacceptable?' To her own ears, the word came out too high and shrill. 'No, just surprising, that's all. Everyone says your career is so important to you. It seems odd that you should decide you could afford such a long break.'

She saw a heavy, faintly cynical smile hover at the corners of his firm lips—lips that she remembered too vividly in very different circumstances.

'My career is important to me,' he nodded. 'That's exactly why I took the time off—but I imagine you're not interested in the full explanation.'

'No, I'm not,' she agreed automatically, and saw that his response to this was veiled suddenly by narrowed eyes and an immobile jaw.

Why had she said that? It was miles from the truth, but she wasn't going to betray that fact to someone who could brush the knowledge of her feelings aside as carelessly as she had brushed aside their week together—and their kiss.

Cleo was suddenly aware that she was cold, standing there on the path. The sun had dropped behind the houses now and a chilly dew was already beginning to fall in the crisp air. Tony suddenly seemed to become aware of this too.

'There's a chill falling—you obviously don't want to be kept out in it. I'll be back at work on Monday, so we'll run into each other then. Nice to see your leg has healed so well.' The words were bland, with an icy thread running through them, and before she could think of a reply in similar vein he had turned and started on his way again, feet pounding the pavement rhythmically in his expensive running shoes.

Cleo opened the gate and walked slowly up the path to their entrance door at the side of the house. She felt quite sick and shaken by the encounter and had to fumble for several futile seconds before her key would fit and turn in the lock. Jane wasn't home as she had an afternoon shift that day, and it was a relief; Cleo needed to be alone to think things out.

But what was there to think? Having sat down with a cup of tea ten minutes later, she was presented forcefully with this question. The whole thing was quite clear, wasn't it? That week in France, and that too-stirring kiss, had definitely meant nothing to him.

At the bottom of her heart she had known that all along, but because she hadn't actually seen him face to face, behaving almost like a stranger, she had been able to dream naïve dreams. Well, now she *had* seen him, and he *had* behaved almost like a stranger, and it was only this development which brought home to her just how rosy some of her dreams of him had become.

And all the while he had been taking that 'extended holiday', sunning himself in Italy and lazily taking in a few of the local attractions—and no doubt these included those made of curvaceous flesh and blood, not just those of wood, paint or stone!

But where did Sir Phineas fit into all this?

'I should have trusted my first impressions of both of them!' Cleo said fiercely aloud to the empty room, and then nearly choked on a gulp of too-hot tea.

She thought back to that evening in December when she had made the acquaintance of each man in very similar circumstances. That should have told her something! Tony with his arrogant, taciturn attitude, making her feel that she was irretrievably in the wrong, contrasted with Sir Phineas's unimpeachable good manners and gallant concern. Why had she ever allowed herself to think anything different? She detested Tony Fitzgerald now, as she should always have done, and that week in France seemed to have been lived by another person, not herself at all!

'Got anything on tonight?' Jane asked casually at five the next evening, which was a rainy one in contrast to yesterday's unusually fine weather.

She had been lounging lazily about the

197

flat in between intermittent bouts of study for most of her day off, but David, the fair-haired physiotherapist, who was practically part of the furniture at Number Three, 36 Charlotte Lane, was collecting her in a few minutes and they were going into town for an early dinner followed by a West End show. Meanwhile, she had brewed some coffee for herself and Cleo, who had just come in from work, a little damp and tired.

'Actually, yes,' said Cleo, trying not to blush and bending down to pull off her shoes to disguise the fact that she undoubtedly was. 'I've been asked out to dinner by Sir Phineas Grimes.' When this announcement was received in total silence, she ventured to look up again. 'Aren't you going to say anything?'

'I'm stunned!'

'Oh gosh, I know—so was I.' Cleo abruptly abandoned her air of sophisticated understatement and bounced down on to the couch beside Jane. 'I don't know what it can possibly mean.'

'It means he's noticed you on the ward, he likes you, he's attracted to you and he wants to take you out and see if there's any future in it,' Jane replied promptly. She wasn't a complicated person, and her own rosy romance with David had followed such a smooth and easy course that she had not made some of the discoveries about love's complexity and men's duplicity that Cleo had recently had cause to explore.

'Do you think so?' Cleo screwed up her face anxiously, torn between feeling thrilled at the prospect and wondering if it was what she really hoped for.

'Well, it's the most usual explanation for a dinner invitation, isn't it?' answered Jane. 'I must say, since we're usually honest with each other, that he's not my type. Not that that means he's awful or anything,' she went on hastily. 'I mean, I hardly know him, but he seems very sophisticated and image-conscious, and frankly, I thought he'd only go for rich young socialites.'

'I know,' nodded Cleo. 'It's making me nervous. I hope he likes what I wear, and that I don't go completely idiotic over him.'

'Of course you won't. Just let him see the real you. He's bound to like that better than any veneer, and if you get to know the real *him*, and like him, then everything will work out fine,' was Jane's confident assurance. David's familiar knock sounded just then, so further discussion was impossible. Jane gulped the last mouthfuls of her coffee and sprang to her feet.

'I must fly,' she said. 'If he comes in and sits down, we'll get talking...and cuddling...and have to bolt our dinner and miss the beginning of the show. But have a great time.'

She planted an impulsive kiss on Cleo's forehead, snatched up her bag and was gone, a ball of happy energy that gave Cleo a momentary pang of envy.

'Why can't things be as simple for me?' she thought restlessly, and found her hand reaching for a non-existent cigarette packet for the first time in weeks.

To shake off the craving, she took a scented soapy bath, although it was too soon to be getting ready for the evening. Sir Phineas was coming at eight—a fashionably late meal, indeed!—and it was not yet even six. Still, there was quite a bit to do, what with washing, conditioning and blow-waving her fine golden-blonde hair, dressing and applying make-up—and something told her that Sir Phineas would expect to see the sophisticated, heavy-eyed evening look, which she wasn't used to, so it would take a bit of time.

By half past seven she was ready, and hoped she looked good enough to please him. The dress, a new one bought only a week ago—as if she had had a premonition that this occasion would arise!—was of smoky sapphire blue crêpe. It moulded closely to the curves of her figure as far as her thighs, but then fell in frothy calf-length folds. The shoulder fastenings were mere thin straps, and followed the diamanté motif of the top of the bodice.

Would she be cold? No. Jane had lent her a black wool coat that couldn't be called glamorous, but was neat, simple and smart, and no doubt any restaurant that Sir Phineas Grimes chose would be quite adequately heated, as would his luxurious car.

There was half an hour in which to relax, but Cleo found it difficult, and she started every time a pair of headlights swept along the street, accompanied by the sound of wheels splashing on the wet road. Fleetingly, it crossed her mind that if it had been Tony Fitzgerald she was waiting for, she would not have felt quite so ill at ease, or quite so apprehensive about whether she would live up to his image and expectations, but she brushed the idea aside.

She never would be waiting to be picked up for an evening with him, for a start, so the whole question of a comparison between the two men was stupid.

At last it came, the smooth sound of the Bentley stopping outside, and then his footsteps crunching on the gravel of the side-path. Cleo was not surprised to find that he had brought flowers—expensive orchids—and he presented them to her

accompanied by a frank glance of apprec-
iation at her closely-sheathed figure, and
a brief kiss on the lips.

So early in the evening! For some reason
this added to the tension she was feeling.
He looked immaculate too, in a black
dinner suit that set off his rich tan and
distinguished silver hair.

He spoke of himself during the purring
car journey, and Cleo was only too pleased
to draw him out. His life would be far
more interesting to talk about than her
own. There was only one ruffle in an
otherwise smooth discussion.

'Don't call me that, for heaven's sake!'
he exploded when she addressed him
tentatively as Sir Phineas. 'Make it Fin,
please!'

'Fin.' She said the name aloud and then
to herself, dazzled by her new permission
to use it. Would she dare to do so on the
ward? 'Fin.' It was quite dashing!

As she had expected, the Mayfair
restaurant he took her to was the last
word in elegance, and it was wonderful to
sweep past the lit-up landmarks of London
on the way, cushioned in the soft leather
seat of the Bentley, and with oceans of leg
room.

The restaurant was full of glamorous
couples, leaning towards each other across
the yellow pools of candlelight that marked

each table. Cleo fleetingly recognised a film star, and a leggy American model with her rock-singer boyfriend. Exalted company indeed!

She remained dazzled by it all for quite some time, and couldn't concentrate on the menu at all. It was a relief, therefore, when Sir Phineas chose and ordered her meal for her—a relief, that was, until she came to her senses as a plate was laid deferentially in front of her and she found it was oysters, a dish she had never been able to stomach at all.

After some heroic, unladylike and unaccustomed gulps of the full-bodied white wine that sparkled in its glass above the white cloth, she managed to slide the slimy creatures down her throat virtually without letting them touch the sides, and the Steak Diane which arrived a short while later was both innocuous and delicious.

Both the wine waiter and Cleo's magnetically attractive companion seemed anxious to keep her glass brimming, and it really was difficult to keep from drinking it as she nodded and smiled in response to his anecdotes of medical and cosmopolitan life.

'He's getting me quite tipsy.' The thought floated hazily through Cleo's consciousness as she embarked upon a mouthwatering cluster of chocolate profiteroles, but somehow she couldn't summon the ability to care. Even the oysters, slipping around somewhere in her digestive system, had ceased to matter.

'Cleo... Liqueurs and coffee?' was Sir Phineas's murmured question after dessert was finished.

'Yes, Fin, that would be lovely.' It seemed the most natural thing in the world to use the dynamic nickname now.

'And a cigarette while we wait?'

'Mmm, lovely,' Of course she was supposed to have given up smoking, but just this once it wouldn't matter.

And there was no harm in a second one to complement the excellent coffee, either. A third *after* the coffee was perhaps going a little too far, but Cleo didn't spend evenings like this every day. She suppressed a small giggle as she thought of how she and her two school friends had started the habit at sixteen, trying to blow smoke-rings, practising a languorous and decadent exhalation, and talking about how they'd be famous actresses or titled wives one day, the centre of attention at fashionable restaurants and nightclubs. Tonight those childish fantasies almost seemed to be coming true...

'How are you enjoying your new job on Coronary Care?' Fin's question recalled her attention to him.

It was the first question he had asked her about herself the entire evening. Not that she'd minded particularly—after all, her own life could scarcely compete with his for glamour and experience.

'Oh, I'm loving it,' she said, deciding not to bother to correct his impression that she'd only just started there. 'It's very rewarding to help patients through such a crisis in their lives. My only regret is that usually they're with us for such a short time, whereas on Women's Medical, where I was before—'

'You're lucky on that ward too, because you come into contact considerably with Tony Fitzgerald,' Sir Phineas interrupted smoothly, making Cleo grow hot with the realisation that she had gone on too long in reply to his question. 'He's a man to watch—headed for a great career. In fact, of course, I've done a lot to encourage him...'

'Have you?'

'Yes, and I think he'll thank me for it one day, though just at the moment I'm a little angry with him.'

'Really?' Guiltily, Cleo knew she was more interested in this discussion of Tony than in anything her companion had said all evening. It surprised her, and roused her a little from the daze into which she was in severe danger of falling.

Surely the sophistication and distinction of a man like Sir Phineas ought to drown out all thought of the Cardiac Registrar. Somehow it didn't, though, and she wanted to hear everything her companion had to say about him.

'Yes, he's postponed sitting for his exams until next year,' Fin explained. 'That kind of thing doesn't look good. The right people would have been impressed if he'd taken them this year.'

'Perhaps he's interested in becoming a better doctor and getting a more solid ground of experience before he goes for the exams, and isn't interested in impressing the right people,' Cleo ventured quietly.

She couldn't help noticing that Sir Phineas's accent had slipped again. Could it really be that the plummy tones were deliberately practised—something he had put on in order to disguise a background he was ashamed of?

'If he's not, he's a fool,' Fin pronounced testily and explosively in answer to Cleo's mild query, making her flinch a little. 'I've told him it's shortsighted and unrealistic to insist on just using "Dr Tony Fitzgerald", and he'll realise it himself when he's older—that it would simply add a distinction...' He finished on an exasperated sigh.

To Cleo it seemed a small thing to make

such a fuss over. 'Anthony' was no doubt more distinguished than plain old 'Tony', but as to it making a difference to the upward path of his career, that seemed unlikely. Her estimation of Sir Phineas dropped a little further and she began to feel, ashamedly, that she might like to go home soon, and that the feelings she had been nurturing for this man all year were really very shallow and silly.

Beyond his technical skills as a doctor, his slightly too smooth good looks, and one or two glamorous accoutrements such as an expensive car, what qualities did he really possess? Snobbery, a fickle taste for beautiful women, and a puffed-up idea of his own importance.

Cleo returned her attention to his stream of words again. Somehow he had got off the subject of Tony and was on to another anecdote relating to himself. She smiled and nodded in the right places, but felt her mind grow hazy once again.

'Time to go, I think.' Fin's drawl cut across her reverie some minutes later. 'Your head is nodding like a yellow poppy-flower.'

He reached a lazy hand across the table and lifted her chin with one finger.

'I'm fine.' It was quite a struggle to reply.

'I'll have you in bed in no time,

kitten,' he said. The double entendre was emphasised by his tone, but Cleo only laughed. Everyone made jokes like that about sex these days.

The walk to the car and the ride home passed in the same haze that had washed over most of the meal, but as they began to cruise through familiar streets, Cleo started to come to herself. She really did feel quite tipsy, and those cigarettes had dizzied her too, now that her body was no longer used to the nicotine.

It had seemed like a wonderful evening at first, under the influence of the moment, but it hadn't really been. She had hardly got a word in edgeways, and Sir Phineas had only that once tried to prompt her into conversation. They hadn't exchanged any opinions or discovered any common interests. They hadn't even laughed much together. Sir Phineas Grimes, when speaking of himself, was usually quite serious.

Cleo risked a glance at the man at her side. His eyes were fixed on the road and she knew he had not seen her shift of gaze. A small smile played around the corners of his lips now. He seemed eager to reach their destination, driving forcefully and negotiating traffic impatiently.

Well, they were almost to Charlotte Lane now. The realisation roused Cleo's energy further. It would be cold after she said goodbye and stepped out of the car.

'Number 36,' Fin announced as he pulled smoothly to a halt at the kerbside directly in front of the house and switched off the engine.

Immediately, before Cleo had had a chance to speak her thanks for the evening, he had leant across and pulled her towards him, kissing her with cool expertise. She had expected it, but not so quickly, nor so mechanically. Her lips responded and in spite of how he had fallen in her estimation, part of her still waited for his touch to arouse her and draw her away into a whirlpool of feeling, but somehow it didn't happen.

Wasn't there something a little *too* practised, too automatic about this man's passion, and about the way he held her—as if he had done it too many times before, with too many different women?

'Fin...'

'Or shall we make it Number 170?'

'I beg your pardon?'

'Your place or mine, darling. I'm finding a variation on the old cliché. 36 or 170?'

Cleo sat back, still in his arms but far enough away to focus her gaze clearly on his face. 'Are you asking me to sleep with you?' The question came out bluntly and she was wide awake and fully in control now.

'Well, no, darling, not *asking*. I assumed we didn't need to have it put into words. I'm simply asking which, in your opinion, would be the better bed.'

He spoke with unswerving confidence and a man-of-the world intonation that suddenly set Cleo's teeth on edge and made her wonder, with a cold sinking in her stomach, what she was doing in this situation. She wasn't the kind of person who did this: she knew that about herself as surely as she knew her own name.

In the moments that passed while she searched for a response that would let him know honestly and carefully how she felt, Jane's earlier words came back to her: 'He wants to see if there's any future in it.'

But Jane had been wrong. Again, Cleo knew this with implacable certainty. This man was not looking for a future, not with someone like her, not after broken marriages with Morgan Fairlane, Lady Helen Trent and Sabrina Tuckett-Ford. He wanted a one-night stand, with someone who would be flattered to the back teeth at the very fact that she was in his bedroom, a pretty little nobody who might give a few hours of pleasure without ever realising how she had been used.

'I'm sorry, I'm not going to bed with

you. It's not something I do.'

'What do you mean, it's not something you *do?*' His eyes glittered darkly, reflecting the faint light of a street lamp.

'I mean I don't like casual affairs. I'm sorry.' But why on earth was she apologising? It wasn't a crime.

'Chloe darling...' He reached out a hand to stop her from drawing away.

'My name is not Chloe. It's Cleo.'

'A little slip of the tongue...' He gave the word a suggestive intonation. 'And you're going to hold it against me.'

His hand reached out again for her, grasping her shoulders with a strength that came only from blind determination to have his own way.

'Please. I'm serious!'

Finally his mood changed.

'I didn't buy you an expensive dinner all for nothing, you common little tease!' The explosion of his anger struck fear into her for a moment and she felt her throat constrict, but then her own anger was aroused and her retort came quickly and icily.

'Didn't you? Then I'm afraid I misunderstood. You should have made the terms of the agreement plainer at the start.'

'Misunderstood! You knew perfectly well what our meal together implied...'

'I didn't.' She cut across his words. 'As

I said before, it was a misunderstanding. If you like simple arrangements, there are women available who lay out the terms of their transactions quite clearly. I suggest you try one, and with any luck you'll find them cheaper, and without wasting all that time over dinner.'

Had she gone too far? Cleo didn't wait to find out. She was out of the car and through the garden gate before she could stop for breath after her blunt words, but her brief fear that he would follow her to continue their confrontation died as she heard the angry roar of the Bentley's engine behind her.

She waited in the bluish darkness of the garden as the car accelerated into the distance. It could be heard all the way up the street, only fading—suddenly—as Sir Phineas braked sharply to turn into his own driveway.

With trembling fingers, Cleo reached for her keys and let herself in. Jane was not home yet, and for the first time the silent flat seemed unsafe. Something creaked, and the shadows of the furniture loomed like human shapes. Quickly her damp hand found the two electric switches beside the door, and with a fumbling movement she flooded the room with light.

It was a relief to hear voices and the clink of crockery faintly through the wall a moment later, coming from the kitchen of the next flat as a man and a woman prepared themselves a late supper. She dropped her silver evening bag on the couch and went into her own kitchen, suddenly thirsty after the oysters, the wine and the salty Steak Diane sauce. A long glass of water followed by a huge cup of scalding tea were what she needed.

She remembered, inconsequentially, that she and Jane had planned to give the kitchen an extra-thorough clean tomorrow. The fridge needed defrosting, and household odds and ends were starting to accumulate on its handy flat top. A friend of Jane's had left a half-smoked packet of cigarettes there the other day, for example.

Cleo knew both that she didn't need one, and that she was going to have one. It had been a horrible end to the evening. Why not set the seal on it? At least it might have a calming effect.

Instinct told her that Sir Phineas would not breathe a word of what had happened. He had too much of a position to maintain, and in any case, despite his anger in the heat of the moment, she knew that for him it was only a minor event, a small impediment to the flow of his will, an irritating incident that was entirely her own fault. She doubted that he would question his own behaviour for an instant.

For herself, it loomed larger, and its effects would last beyond tomorrow, when no doubt her mouth would taste bitterly of ash and her body would feel lethargic and abused. Yesterday she had seen Sir Phineas's lordly and unexpected interest as an antidote to the hurt and anger caused by Tony Fitzgerald's surprise reappearance.

To-day, it seemed part of her confused feelings about the Registrar from Coronary Care. If Sir Phineas Grimes could expect her to regard a night of complete physical passion so lightly, then of course Tony Fitzgerald could kiss her warmly and dizzyingly without a question of emotion entering into the matter.

She had been an absolute naïve fool not to have known that from the beginning, and if Tony—heaven forbid—should ever find out just how strongly that kiss had affected her, he would scarcely be able to believe it.

CHAPTER NINE

'It's good to have Tony back on the ward again, isn't it?' Angie Carruthers remarked to Cleo several days later as they sat over their evening meal in the staff dining-room.

'Yes, lovely.'

Cleo's bright smile did not reach her eyes and her enthusiastic nod was a little forced. Fortunately Angie had slipped into a dreamy state and didn't seem to have noticed. There was a contented smile hovering at the corner of her prettily-shaped mouth as she cut fastidious morsels of chicken, broccoli and potatoes.

There had recently been some kind of *coup d'état* in the large hospital kitchens. Several new faces had appeared and the food had suddenly got better again. In fact, this chicken dish was quite delicious, and *not* swimming in fat as it would have been under the previous régime, but Cleo's enjoyment of it was spoiled by her reading of Angie's expression.

It was Tony Fitzgerald himself who was responsible for the dreaminess and contentment. Were they involved together? Perhaps not yet, but Cleo knew that Angie expected and wanted it to happen.

She was a nice enough girl, though she lacked humour, and Cleo's angry outburst several months ago, the day before she left for that memorable skiing holiday, had not after all ripened into enmity between them, but all the same the two were not close friends. Probably Angie was not the sort of girl who gathered a close collection of female friends.

She was a little too complacent in her awareness of her own good looks, and was mostly to be found at a table with several men when she ate here in the dining-room, quietly enjoying their attempts to outshine each other in gaining her interest. She had been out with several doctors at the hospital, but there was something new in the way she seemed to be considering Tony, wasn't there? As if she'd already decided that he was going to be more serious.

Or was that simply Cleo's jaundiced perception, created by those feelings inside her that still wouldn't go away in spite of everything?

'His holiday seems to have done him good,' she ventured, hating the fact that she couldn't resist trying to keep his name in the conversation.

'Hasn't it, though?' Angie agreed. 'I told him he should drop out of medicine and out of English society altogether and become an Italian fisherman.'

She glanced briefly around the dining-hall, clearly looking for him, but the two nurses from Coronary Care had been sent off for an early meal and there were not yet many other people eating. With a shaft of late afternoon sun breaking through some clouds and lighting up dust motes and the metal of cutlery, trolleys and table-legs, it was easy to take in the room at a glance. Tony was not there. Angie returned her attention to her meal, obviously disappointed.

'I hadn't realised he'd tan so heavily,' said Cleo. In a minute it would be quite obvious why she was trying to keep this conversation alive. Her face would betray her somehow—with a blush or would-be casual expression that was too carefully put on.

'Yes, it suits him marvellously well, doesn't it?' said Angie, again with that smile almost of ownership. 'It makes Fin Grimes's look a bit artificial—which it is.'

'*Is* it?' And Angie had called him 'Fin' too! She seemed to have inside information about both the men who had figured in Cleo's life this year.

''Fraid so. Half bottle, half lamp.' Angie gave a wicked laugh.

'So you don't have a very high opinion of Sir Phineas,' Cleo ventured next.

'On the contrary. I think he's a divine man. And of course *no one* denies he's a wonderful doctor. Even his conceit is part of his charm when you get to know him a bit better.'

'As you obviously do,' Cleo nodded.

'We went out together a few times,' Angie admitted. 'He's fun. We went to some amazing places. I even got my picture

217

in the social pages!'

And that event was evidently worth the price that Cleo had no doubt Angie had paid for it. The dark-haired nurse looked up in response to Cleo's silence following the announcement, and she recollected herself hastily.

'How thrilling for you!'

'Yes, it was—although you seem a bit doubtful.'

'Oh, it's not that,' Cleo assured her quickly. 'It's just...well, to be quite honest, casual affairs aren't quite my style.'

'Oh well, you know with a man like Fin that that's all it's going to be,' Angie replied calmly. 'I enjoyed it. I wasn't in any danger of getting emotionally involved. He's rather badly between wives at the moment, of course, poor love, but I had no illusions that he'd ever pick a *nurse* for anything serious.'

'No, of course not,' Cleo murmured mechanically.

She could not imagine ever being able to speak in that flippant, casual way about someone who had been her lover. It made her even more certain that Angie expected to be safely in Tony's arms soon and that was why the pretty nurse could now dismiss 'Fin' so easily.

As for Cleo, she wondered now how she could ever have found the man attractive.

He had gone back to his old way of relating to her on the ward now, since Saturday's stormy interchange—the same bland, brilliant smile, the same velvet-toned thanks for coffee or other nursing assistance—and Cleo did not regret this development one bit.

Then something else struck her. Angie had given the word 'nurse' a sneering intonation that distorted her pretty feature momentarily. Did she actually despise her own profession? Did she think that Sir Phineas was right to divide women into two classes like that? The ones you married—with a name and position as well as beauty—and then the ones you merely took to bed, pretty but unimportant? It was positively feudal!

Cleo's indignation was all the more pronounced because she was guiltily aware that she had come close to sharing the man's attitude. She had felt flattered at his having plucked her from oblivion and installed her at his side for that expensive evening, had been terrified that she would not prove worthy, had tried to appear and be sophisticated and a woman of the world in a way that she was not, and did not, she knew now, even want to be.

'I can see you disapprove.' Angie was still studying her.

'Not about you having...going out with

him,' said Cleo. She decided to be truthful, but at the same time fair, if she could. 'But I think it's nonsense about nurses being too inferior for someone like him, and I'm surprised you can condone that.'

She reached into her bag for matches and cigarettes as she spoke, lighting one in an expert and habitual gesture. The packet had been new at lunchtime and already there were only twelve left. She had been smoking regularly since Saturday's outing, unable to fight against the need in spite of the unworded disappointment in Jane's expression each time she lit one up.

'Oh well...you have to be realistic,' Angie was saying with a shrug.

Yes, you did have to be realistic. Tony didn't care, never had and never would. Cleo had no will-power and was doomed to be a smoker till the end of her days. Someone coughed behind her at the next table and she jumped guiltily, although this was the section of the dining-hall where smoking was permitted.

Only last week she had been in the camp of the non-smokers, finding Shirley Byrne's constant puffing a violation of the clean air she had come to enjoy, and now here she was doing the same thing herself. It seemed to echo the rapid and inconsistent change in her feelings about Sir Phineas Grimes and Tony Fitzgerald somehow.

'Tony! Over here!' Angie's whole attitude had suddenly changed. Her shoulders had been set in a slightly defensive way after those last few moments of conversation with Cleo, but now they were relaxed lazily and confidently against the hard curved back of the chair.

'Hullo, Angie...'

Cleo's back was towards him and she knew he hadn't seen her. When he did, as he stepped past Angie's chair to sit down beside the dark-haired girl, the change in his expression was unmistakable. A mask of polite neutrality descended, blotting out the very evident pleasure that had been his response to Angie.

'Hullo, Cleo,' he said.

'Oh, hi!' The words came out with a brittle inflection. She stubbed out her cigarette quickly, after a last intake of smoke and nicotine, which had doubtless narrowed her eyes and set her cheeks in unattractive planes—not that that would make any difference to his feeling, or lack of it, for her. 'Excuse me, I'd better get back to the ward.'

It wasn't at all necessary to hurry. She and Angie had left the ward together, and the pretty brown-eyed nurse was still sitting there as if she had all the time in the world. There was another ten whole minutes, in

221

fact, before there was the slightest risk of being late back.

Angie didn't comment on Cleo's sudden haste, however, and it was clear that she was quite happy to be left alone with Tony. When Cleo instinctively and furtively glanced back at the pair on reaching the doorway of the dining-hall, they appeared to be already locked in animated conversation.

'Back early, Staff?' queried Sister Hennessy, slightly surprised.

'Oh...yes, I was worried about Mrs Packer,' Cleo improvised quickly.

'Really?' the lively older nurse exclaimed with a sharp, automatic glance across to Cleo's elderly widowed patient, whose small frame was quite dwarfed by the medical equipment that surrounded her. 'You said she was fine before tea, that's why I asked you to go off first with Angie, rather than sending one of the third-years.'

'Oh, I mean, it's just that she's such a sweetie,' Cleo said hastily. 'And she seems so lonely. I didn't want to have to leave her for too long.'

Fortunately, it could easily have been the truth. Daisy Packer was one of the nicest-natured patients Cleo had come across in a long while, never making demands, always thoughtful of staff and fellow patients even in the extremity of her illness, and yet never tainting this selflessness with the pose of martyrdom that some people could adopt.

Sister Hennessy accepted the reason that Cleo had offered.

'Yes, she's a treasure, isn't she? She's pining for her husband, but she's not someone to lie down and die just because he's gone.'

'I'm sure she hasn't had an easy life, either,' Cleo said. 'Eight children, yet only one of them's left in London to be near her—although the others have all done well in their lives elsewhere.'

'She's seen that you're back,' Sister Hennessy put in. 'Go and ask her if there's anything special she wants, or if there's anything wrong. She's the type that always says nothing rather than running the risk of being a nuisance.'

Cleo went, glad to be able to become immersed in concern for another person again. Now that she knew Tony was working tonight, it would be difficult not to think of him, difficult not to look up expecting to see him every time the door opened.

He did come in twice during the evening. The first time was at about nine, when the third-year student on the other side of the ward picked up a disturbing trend in her patient's hourly rhythm strips, and Sister Hennessy thought a change in Mr McPherson's medication might be necessary.

In fact, Tony decided that it was not, and would have been gone again in only a few minutes except that he decided to come over to Cleo's side of the ward.

'Everything all right with Mrs Packer, Staff?' he asked her casually, his wide shoulders seeming relaxed and capable as ever.

'Yes, she's settled down now,' nodded Cleo, presenting an outward calm that she could never genuinely feel in this man's presence now.

Her eyes skated away from any contact with his own as soon as it threatened to occur. Why was it so impossible not to be aware of him, after one kiss, and so long ago? Was it just that his touch had stirred surprising physical depths? She gathered her breath in unsteadily to go on speaking.

'Earlier she was restless and depressed, I think,' she said.

'Her husband died of a coronary thrombosis.' Tony spoke thoughtfully, his grey-blue eyes fixed on the patient now, as if he too was glad to be able to look away. 'That probably makes it harder for her. This ward would be a reminder of his death as much as of her own mortality.'

'Yes, that's true. I hadn't thought of it like that,' Cleo nodded.

He moved on—two beds down, to where Angie Carruthers' patient was—after this, and Cleo allowed herself, but only for a moment, to look at his retreating figure.

At the beginning of the year she would have been cynically surprised that he had shown the human concern he had just revealed. To have remembered the cause of Mr Packer's death and put it into the emotional context of his widow's illness was not something every doctor would have done. But Tony seemed to have changed and softened so much over these past months. Was that simply Cleo's own perception, clouded by her confused feelings? Or was it that she had come to know the real Tony during that timeless interlude in France?

Or was there another reason for the change? When he appeared on the ward only minutes before the nursing shift was due to end, Cleo thought she had the answer to her question.

Because there was no good reason for him to turn up again. Everything was in order. The ward was very quiet and only dimly lit now. Every now and then a nurse's quiet rhythmic footfalls padded across the parquet floor, and there were occasional murmuring voices because the night nursing staff had arrived for change-over.

No one had called Tony. He made a quick round of the beds, ostensibly checking that his earlier decision not to alter Mr McPherson's medication had been the correct one, and instructing Night Sister to report any further change straight away.

'Although of course I'm only second on call,' Cleo heard him say.

Then as if casually, and almost by accident, he arrived at Angie Carruthers' bed and began to talk to her, in a low voice that Cleo shamelessly tried to hear but could not. He was probably waiting for the dark-haired nurse to finish work, and they would leave the hospital together.

Yes, Cleo's earlier question was answered. It was Angie Carruthers who had brought about the change in Tony. Perhaps their interest in each other dated from the beginning of the year, and it was only Tony's absence in France and Italy which had stopped their relationship from flowering long ago. In fact she now remembered that odd time when Tony had asked her if she knew why Angie had paged him several times when not much was really wrong. It was clear now that that had been a signal of Angie's interest,

226

and that Tony had picked up on it.

'I'll look after her specially well. She's a love, isn't she?' Marian Peterson was saying. She was the nurse who was to take Cleo's place with Mrs Packer for the night.

'She is,' nodded Cleo, trying to forget about Tony.

'Are you on tomorrow afternoon?' Staff Nurse Peterson asked.

'Yes.'

'See you then, then.'

'Yes, goodnight,' replied Cleo, repressing a sigh.

It was a relief to be outside. The night air struck crisply against her hot cheeks and refreshed her tired body. She had walked to the hospital this afternoon, enjoying the exercise, and planned now to sit in the shelter outside the hospital gate and wait for a bus to get her home again. There would probably be one or two other nurses waiting there too, for comfort and safety.

'Cleo! Wait!'

Running footsteps, of which she had been dimly conscious in the back of her mind as she walked, resolved themselves into those of Tony Fitzgerald, and before Cleo could think of hurrying on and pretending she hadn't heard, he was at her side.

Not only that, he had reached a warm

hand to her shoulder in a gesture that was partly restraining, partly—unless this was simply wishful thinking—caressing. Instinctively, before Cleo could repress her body's need for him, she had relaxed against the hand instead of shaking it off. Quickly, though, she pulled herself together.

'What do you want?' Her question was deliberately abrupt and she kept walking at a steady pace, rigid after nearly betraying herself at his touch.

'Don't you think we need to talk?' His voice was pitched low, as if he was afraid that other hospital staff on their way off duty might interrupt or overhear them.

'No, I don't,' she blurted stupidly. What was she trying to do? Keep him from guessing how vulnerable she was to him, of course, but the blunt blocking of everything he said wasn't the way to go about it.

'Well, I do.' His retort was controlled, but betrayed some deeper feeling. Was it anger? Impatience? His hand had slid down to grasp her arm—not flesh, but the wool of the navy cape that protected her upper body from the night air, which was chilly. At first he was pulling her back, but then he seemed to relent and started to match his pace to hers. 'Yes, you're right. We might as well keep walking, because here's scarcely the place for it.'

'For what?'

'How were you getting home?' He ignored her question.

'By bus.'

'I'll drive you.'

By this time she could no longer bring herself to argue simply for the sake of establishing distance between them, and in any case it had just begun to drizzle—only a fine mist of dampness as yet, but no doubt it would soon be torrenting down.

'Very well, then,' she said.

Silence fell after this. Whatever it was that he had to say, there was evidently to be no leading up to it as they walked to the car-park, and no small talk either, because if he didn't initiate any, Cleo certainly wasn't going to. The rain was coming down more heavily now, as she had foreseen, and Tony quickened his pace, reaching a low-slung dark-blue sports car and swinging open the door for her just as she arrived.

'My shoes are all muddy,' she said shortly, hesitating.

'Don't worry about that, for heaven's sake. I'll be getting it cleaned soon anyway.' He leaned across to pull her in, then shut the door impatiently, and Cleo realised that her hesitation had simply allowed rain to splash on the leather seats.

'It's a lovely car. Sorry, the seat's a bit...'

'Only second-hand.' He cut across her apology, and had already revved the engine impatiently into life.

Cleo remembered that he was second on call tonight. He was probably afraid that whatever he had to say to her would be interrupted by his beeper sounding. And she was more sure than ever that he had been intending to drive Angie home until he had seen herself leaving the ward. Did he feel he had to tell her in plain words that their time in France together had meant nothing?

Probably he did, simply because it was so painfully obvious that she was still cherishing the memory of it all. Well, she'd soon convince him that words weren't necessary.

The car was like a tiny cocoon of warmth and darkness moving through the wet night. Tony drove smoothly, giving the impression of both speed and safety. Cleo felt drained and tired and might have enjoyed surrendering herself to the hypnotic sound of the wipers and nodding into a doze if it had been anyone but Tony at the wheel. As it was, she sat stiffly, waiting and dreading for him to speak.

'I don't suppose you've got a cigarette on you, by any chance?' The question, flung at her suddenly and without preamble, was the last thing she would have expected.

'A cigarette!' The exclamation came out squeaky with amazement. 'But...you don't smoke...'

'I used to. I stopped at the end of last year.'

'Then why do you want...?'

'I'd like one. I feel like one. No reason,' he offered tersely.

'Don't,' she blurted out before she could stop herself, then went on hastily as she caught his surprised expression. 'Honestly, you'll regret it. Just one and you'll be right back up to how much you smoked before. That's what happened to me, just since last Saturday, and I regret it so much... Why are you slowing down?'

She broke off the tumbled speech as she became aware that the car had slackened to a halt.

'Because this is your place, isn't it?' He smiled drily and crookedly, revealing slightly uneven white teeth.

'Oh.' Cleo looked out through the blur of water on the windows. 'Yes, of course.'

'So could I have that cigarette?'

Silently she reached into her bag for the compact box. Just the feel of its neat cardboard shape had sometimes been a comfort to her in the past during stressful moments. That was addiction for you.

231

'Thank you,' he said, pressing the automatic lighter on the dashboard as she handed him the packet.

'Is this the first one you've had since you gave up?' she asked, not caring if he thought her presumptuous or puritanical.

'As a matter of fact, yes.'

'And how many used you to smoke?'

'Up to two packets a day.'

'Gosh!'

'Started in my sinful student days, like a lot of people,' Tony explained, relaxing back in his seat.

Cleo found she was doing the same. The curved bucket-style shape was very cosy and comfortable. The leather was rather worn in parts, unlike the glossy perfection of the upholstery in Sir Phineas's Bentley. Surprisingly, she decided she liked the worn look better.

'Medicine's a tough course, no doubt about it,' Tony was saying. 'And I was pushed—and pushed myself—quite hard. Cigarettes helped, though some mornings I'd wake up feeling as though someone had been burning a rubber tyre in my mouth after an all-night study binge.'

'I know the feeling,' Cleo laughed.

She noticed that the automatic light had clicked out, signifying that the wire coil inside was ready, but Tony hadn't reached for it. It would have cooled down again

232

in another minute and he'd have to press it again. Still, he seemed to have lost his impatient need to hurry. How unexpected that they should be talking easily and naturally to one another again, almost as they had in France, and about smoking of all things! She remembered their first clash on the ward, just as he referred to it himself.

'...But it took me a while to finally wake up to the fact that it was hypocritical—lecturing my heart patients about their bad habits, then going off and filling my own lungs with tar,' he told her. 'I stopped just before Christmas—and barged around like a bear with a sore head for the next two months. I couldn't even look at someone smoking without going off. You came in for a share of that. Do you remember?'

'Yes, I do,' laughed Cleo, and her cheeks grew warm. There was something in his intonation when he said 'Do you remember?' The way two lovers reminded each other of moments in their relationship. But no, that was only the way *she* felt, nothing to do with him at all.

'I was longing for a cigarette that day in the ward kitchen, and there you were, puffing contentedly away...'

They laughed again, and Cleo relaxed a little more. In another moment he would ask her if she'd disliked him then. She would say that she had, but then he would ask about the change that had happened in France. She would confess how much his kiss had meant, and then...

Then he'd apologise for it, or something, embarrassed at her show of emotion. He would say he'd meant to make it clear that he didn't want her to take it too seriously, was sorry if she'd misunderstood. Probably the way she was lolling in the curved seat, aware of her body and of his so close by, was already making him uneasy. She sat up stiffly again, looking towards the cigarette lighter.

'So are you going to have one of my cigarettes, or shall I put them away?' There! That was a nice matter-of-fact tone, betraying nothing.

'Actually I won't have one after all,' he said, flinging a brief surprised glance in her direction.

The rain had eased now, and it was bright enough in the car for his features to be visible as they had not been a few moments ago. Somehow the rain-washed darkness had made things easier, and now the unfiltered presence of the fluorescent street-lamp was intrusive.

'For one thing, there may not be time,' Tony was continuing. 'I'm on call, as I suppose you know.'

'Yes,' she nodded.

'And secondly, of course, you're right. It's easy to believe that I've kicked the habit and can afford one tiny relapse—but why tempt fate? Are you having one?'

'Not now,' said Cleo.

'But don't whip yourself over the fact that you've started again, Cleo. It can happen to anyone.' He gripped her hand in a sudden gesture of support and she inched away from the power of his firm-muscled touch. Fortunately, Tony misinterpreted the gesture and took his hand away again. 'You'll kick it again soon, and this time it'll be for good.'

'This is starting to sound like a Smokers Anonymous meeting,' Cleo remarked, deliberately flippant, though her heart was beating faster.

'Yes, it is,' he laughed, tilting his head back against the seat for a moment and narrowing his grey-blue eyes.

It was obvious that he was preparing to say something, and Cleo realised that this entire conversation had not been the thing that was filling most of his thoughts. It had been a way of preparing her, of finding some common ground before he arrived at his real reason for wanting to speak with her. In fact, was it unreasonably suspicious of her to wonder if the subject of smoking had been deliberately engineered by that first request for a cigarette? Had he wanted to create the illusion that they shared some feelings and experiences, so that when he let her down gently, as he was about to do, she would not feel entirely bereft?

'Tony...'

'Yes, Cleo?'

'If you... I mean, did you want to say something special to me?'

Of all the wordings to choose! 'Something special' sounded like a proposal of marriage! To make it clear that she had not meant that, or anything like it, she slid her back around so that it was pressing—very uncomfortably—against the door of the car. There! She had created as much physical distance between them as it was possible to do inside the confined space of this car.

Tony had not spoken yet, but no doubt it was only Cleo's heightened awareness in his presence which elongated seconds into minutes and made the silence seem dense with meaning.

Then suddenly it was no longer silent, and the small car was filled with the piercing electronic rhythm of Tony's beeper. He reached into the pocket of his blue shirt, where the object was clipped, and switched it off, muttering an indistinguishable oath at the same time.

Cleo reached for the door handle. Clearly this intrusion of professional responsibility signalled an end to their talk, whatever he had intended to say to her.

'I'm going away for two weeks from tomorrow,' Tony said quickly. 'A conference in Edinburgh and then some research. Damn! Look—you went out with Fin Grimes last week, didn't you?'

'Yes... If that's any of your business,' Cleo replied, goaded by his blunt tone, and desolated, in spite of everything, at the realisation that Tony was to disappear from her life again, if only for two weeks.

'It isn't my business,' he agreed, his accent stronger than usual. 'Unless...but no, this isn't the time for it.' She couldn't tell if he was speaking to her, or merely thinking aloud. 'It's just that if I were you, I wouldn't expect anything to come of it.'

'No—well, I'm not completely naïve,' retorted Cleo, thinking of the lessons she felt she had learnt over the past months—that kisses and complete lovemaking, even in an apparently romantic and genuine setting, could mean nothing at all.

'Good...' His lids were hooded suddenly and his drawling tone concealed an emotion she could not fathom. 'Well, I'm glad the warning was unnecessary.'

'Thank you for the ride home.' Cleo intended to make this a departing line, but her movement of the door handle only created an ineffectual click.

'There's a trick to it.' Tony leaned past her and she felt the pressure of his shoulder against hers and saw the bare muscular column of his neck only inches from her face.

The door fell open a little, letting in a thin cold breath of damp air, and his weight dropped into the driver's seat again. Like the time they had said goodbye in France, this was another of the moments where time seemed to stretch for Cleo and she was aware of everything that happened as if it passed before her eyes in slow motion.

Tony's left arm lay along the seat behind her, and his right, after opening the door, came to her face, his dry, smooth fingertips brushing across her cheek in a soft, deliberate caress that turned her to face him. Wordlessly, as if he knew she would not protest, he moulded his arms around her and brought his mouth to hers, parting her lips against his own and kissing her sweetly and breathtakingly.

It was so strange that he could both draw from her a response of intense physical passion and longing, and create within her a feeling of security and ease that felt like entering safe harbour after a storm at sea.

Cleo sighed against him, and felt his breathing growing more rapid now against the soft swell of her breasts. His hands were caressing her, in curving rhythmic movements that made her glimpse truly for the first time what a complete exploration of her own sensuality could be like with a man such as Tony, a man who possessed both strength and sensitivity in large measure.

If it hadn't been for that wretched call to the hospital, which she knew must be in his mind and which he would have to act on at any moment, what would she have done? Invited him in, gone through the motions of a late-night cup of coffee, and then...

She came to her senses and pulled away with a suddenness that left her bereft and numb. She could see that Tony was struggling for control, his eyes narrow, hard and fathomless.

A gust of wind caught at the car door and wrenched it open, flooding the interior with frigid air and a spattering of the rain which had just started again.

With a flash of insight, Cleo could see what the whole episode meant now. Tony's warning about Sir Phineas had been equally a warning that she should not take his own lovemaking too seriously either. She had seen his change of mood after her comment that she wasn't as naïve as he seemed to think. If she hadn't taken his kiss too much to heart in France, then he could afford another one, another piece of easy pleasure, equally without meaning.

And as for her own response... She understood how easy it would be to give in to someone when she felt so strongly. It had been easy to refuse Fin Grimes's unattractive proposal, because he had had no real power over her heart or her senses, but tonight, with Tony, it was different, and that made it all the more vital to protect her vulnerability.

She must never open herself to the risk of giving in to these feelings for him because she knew, as she suddenly knew indisputably that she loved him, that he did not and would never feel the same way. Before he could speak, which she sensed he was about to do, she had to set the seal on her new determination.

'Hadn't you better get back to the hospital?' she said harshly, and left the car, crossing the dark wet lawn to the house through the thickening rain.

CHAPTER TEN

'Letters for you, readdressed from the hospital. Sorry they're wet,' said Jane, tossing down a pile of four white envelopes, dampened at the edges by rain.

Cleo glanced at them from her position by the stove, keeping vigil over a saucepan of milk that she was heating to make hot chocolate drinks, while her thoughts were occupied in travelling a familiar circular pattern—revolving around Tony, of course.

The top letter, and the soggiest, was a bank statement, and no doubt the others were similarly unimportant. They could wait until they dried out a bit.

After a promising spring, summer seemed to have gone on strike, and Cleo had woken morning after morning to the sound of water rattling metallically down the drainpipe outside her window. It was late afternoon, and Jane had just returned from early shift, bedraggled but pink-cheeked after dashing from the bus.

Cleo had had a quiet day off, writing to her sister and to her parents to arrange a couple of days down in Devon with them soon. Ten days had passed since she had sat with Tony in his car, and of course, since he had been away, she had not seen him. The memory of his kiss remained as a draining, almost physical thing which had the power to suddenly sweep over her without warning—as it was doing now—making her wonder how mere memory could be so strong.

There had only been one positive result from that evening. She had stopped smoking again, though it was more out of a determination to prove to herself that she was as strong-willed as he was than anything else.

'Hot chocolate?' she asked Jane, shaking off the thoughts.

'Yes, *please!*'

'I thought you'd need it. *I* don't, but I'm succumbing anyway,' Cleo said, her golden voice a dry drawl.

'Oh, come on, Cleo! You've been to the gym or jogging practically every day for weeks now, haven't you?'

'True. But it seems to take two hours to exercise off one slice of bread. I couldn't get down to size ten in a million years.'

'Because your body's not made to be size ten,' Jane pointed out truthfully. 'It's a natural size twelve. Your figure's lovely now, and if you lost much more weight you'd start to look *too* thin.'

'Someone very famous said that a woman could never be too rich or too thin, didn't they?' Cleo retorted.

'Well, whoever it was was wrong on both counts,' was Jane's emphatic opinion. 'If some of those top models these days were cats, we'd all be ringing the RSPCA. And from their pictures in magazines, heiresses look like a collection of boring little snoots.'

'OK, OK!' Cleo's bright laugh filled the

kitchen. The argument was restoring her good humour. 'I'll be content with size twelve and a bicycle instead of a Rolls.'

'Well, from what you told me about your dinner with Sir Phineas, his Bentley wasn't worth the price of his company,' observed Jane, narrowing her eyes and inhaling with relish as she took the large mug of foaming pinkish chocolate from Cleo and pressed her red-tipped fingers gratefully around its warm sides.

'True,' Cleo nodded briefly. She'd told Jane something about her evening with Sir Phineas, of course, but by no means everything. Fortunately, it was easy to skim over details with Jane these days, as she was so immersed in David whenever she wasn't working or studying.

'By the way, I've been meaning to mention... I've noticed Tony Fitzgerald is back.' Jane suddenly veered on to this unexpected tack, taking Cleo by surprise.

'Oh, yes... Only he's away at the moment.'

'Yes, Shirley Byrne told me so at lunch.'

'You sat next to Shirley?'

'Credit thy friend with sense, O doubting one. *She* sat next to me. To extract information, of course.' Jane frowned delicately. 'She's an odd girl.'

'She is,' Cleo nodded. 'But what was the information?'

'Well, I don't think I gave it to her,' explained Jane. 'Basically, she was grilling me about Tony. You see, to be fair, I think she's quite lonely. She's an only child, apparently, and her parents are quite elderly, and I think she just doesn't really have much of an idea of how to make friendships with people. She plays all these clumsy games, and vicious little teases that are designed to be jokes, only they backfire. Remember your Valentine's Day card?'

'Do I ever!' grimaced Cleo.

'Well, perhaps I'm wrong, but I think she might have been trying to say to you, "Hands off, I want him!" with all that, though it's a weird way to go about it.'

'I don't think she's got a chance with Tony,' Cleo heard herself put in brightly.

'Why? Have you ensnared him with your charms?'

'No, of course not!' Cleo turned to the sink and started to fill the milk saucepan with water, to hide her hot cheeks, but Jane remained unsuspecting.

'I'm only joking, silly. I know you can't stand him. I presume that's why his name hasn't so much as crossed your lips for weeks, and am respecting your desire to endure him in silence.'

Under cover of the water churning into the saucepan, Cleo sighed. Now was the moment for a confession and a heart-to-heart talk, but she wasn't going to confess her new feelings. It wasn't that Jane wouldn't understand and wouldn't be sympathetic, but in a moment of self-knowledge Cleo realised that she felt excluded by her friend's happiness in love.

Jane had a new perspective now, and the time was past when they could sigh over roguish young housemen together, or over a face glimpsed in the street. Jane would see the situation through the rosy spectacles of her own feelings. Of course it wasn't that Cleo did not want her friend to be happy, but she felt she had taken another step into full maturity now that she had realised that someone's happiness could close doors as well as open them.

'Anyway, you haven't told me what Shirley was wanting to find out,' she made herself say cheerfully, because she knew her silence was unnatural.

'Oh, just whether Tony's involved with anyone else, I think,' Jane said, brushing damp hair off her forehead with her small hand. 'And I couldn't be much help, because I didn't have the slightest idea.'

'Well, if she asks again, tell her it's Angie Carruthers.' Cleo's flippancy had a forced note to her own ears, but it passed without comment from Jane.

'Is it really?' Jane was merely interested in the news as gossip. 'I thought she was still playing the field while she waited for some wealthy private patient to tumble for her.'

'You're underestimating her,' said Cleo, though it was an effort to be just. 'She's a nice girl, with a lot to offer.'

'And the offer's been accepted?'

'Any day now, I'd say.'

Oh, she hated talking like this about it, and now, thank goodness, Jane had finished her chocolate and scraped back the chair to get to her feet.

'Anyway, it's about time I peeled off this uniform,' she decided. 'It feels as if it's about to graft itself to my skin. Want me to rinse the cups?'

'No, of course not. Let's leave them till later.'

'Oh dear! No housewifely instincts at all!' giggled Jane, and left the kitchen.

Cleo turned to the pile of letters on the pale-varnished wooden table. Yes, a bank statement, a glossy brochure offering discount vouchers at a local department store, and then two addressed by hand in unfamiliar block capitals.

Or *were* they unfamiliar? Impatiently, Cleo tore off the corners and slid her thumb across the fold, making an untidy tear. They both had Italian stamps, and were postcards, though they had been sealed inside envelopes. And the scrawled signature on each was the same: 'Tony.'

Strength suddenly drained from Cleo's legs and she had to sit down, pulling back the chair awkwardly from the table. So he had written to her! And by some terrible stroke of luck the letters had got lost in the postal system and only turned up now, months later. The Italian mail service was said to be inefficient...or could there be another reason?

Cleo remembered the day that Shirley Byrne had been hanging around the hospital letter rack. Was it too far-fetched to suspect her of having sabotaged...? Surely not!

And yet, as she and Jane had just agreed, the narrow-eyed nurse did have an odd approach to life, and no real sense of the fitness of things. What, in another person, would have seemed like unforgivable deceitfulness seemed almost pitiful in Shirley, as if the girl really didn't have much idea of how to deal with other human beings in an acceptable way.

Anyhow, the damage was done now. Whether it was by the international postal system, or by Shirley Byrne, was immaterial. And after all, perhaps the postcards would have made no real difference to how things stood between herself and Tony.

Having decided this, Cleo could at last manage to actually read them.

'Things felt flat after you left,' began the first one, dated only a few days after her departure. 'I'm sure you know why.'

Her heart lurched as she read the words. It was a reference to their kiss, wasn't it? And didn't it suggest that he had thought of it as a beginning to something, not as a meaningless moment? She kept reading. He talked about his reasons for deciding to stay away so long, sketching a vivid impression of how he had pushed himself almost to breaking point in his work, and saying how it was only by taking a break to go skiing that he had realised he wanted to take things more slowly.

'I'll be away for nearly two months,' he wrote, then finished, 'I hope my reasons make sense to you. If we were talking, I could make it clearer. Here's an address if you'd like to write...' The name and address of a *pensione* followed.

Slowly Cleo replaced the card—a glossily printed view of Rome by night—in its envelope. It was more than just a casual card, wasn't it? Reading between the lines, hadn't he been asking her to respond in kind to the small step towards intimacy that he had taken?

She took out the second card, a blue-toned ocean view, written several weeks later, and cooler in tone, more of the 'Having a wonderful time' variety. Because he'd been waiting for a reply from her and hadn't got one, of course.

For one mad moment Cleo wanted to get a message to him—in Edinburgh, he'd said, hadn't he?—to say that it was all a mistake, and she would have written straight away only she'd never got the cards, but it wasn't too late, was it...?

Then she realised how useless that would be, because by now it *was* too late. That card had not been a declaration of love, merely an expression of potential interest. Her silence had been taken as a rejection, and of course by now he had turned his interest elsewhere. To Angie Carruthers, in fact, and she was obviously rewarding him with the kind of response that would soon turn into love.

Cleo's chance was now irrevocably lost in the past, and she could scarcely blame Tony for it. After only one kiss, no one could be expected to wait for very long. By now he would only be embarrassed if she told him how seriously she'd taken the whole thing, how strongly she felt about him.

As for that second kiss last week, the two postcards didn't change its meaning.

Or rather, lack of meaning. It was quite possible that Tony still felt a sexual attraction for her, which might flare in the intimacy of a place like his car, but if he was looking for anything more than that, it was with Angie.

'I'm worried about my patient's ectopic beat.'

It was some days later, and Angie Carruthers had crossed over to Cleo to murmur her doubt. The ward was quiet this week, with only four beds occupied. Plump, bossy Sister Grieve was off for her break—a late one—at the moment.

'Why, what's wrong?' Cleo tried to sound cheerful and normal, and she met Angie's worried gaze steadily, though it was hard to behave naturally towards the pretty dark-haired nurse these days. The two-day retreat at her parents' place in Devon during her last days off had helped to put things in perspective at the time, but now that she was back on the ward with Angie, and aware that Tony Fitzgerald had returned to work too, her hopeless feelings had returned stronger than ever.

'It's increased in frequency,' said Angie. 'I think I should call Dr Fi...call the Night Registrar.'

She had caught back Tony's name, but not quite in time, and she looked a little guilty when she saw that Cleo had noticed it.

'Oh, Dr Fitzgerald's on tonight, is he?' she said smoothly, hiding an anger which she felt she might be justified in expressing. Was Alan Tandred's ectopic beat really more frequent, or was Angie Carruthers just using it as an excuse to summon Tony to the ward? And was it just a coincidence that Sister was absent at the moment, so she couldn't be consulted about what was necessary? 'I suppose you'd like me to check?'

'Yes, if you don't mind,' Angie nodded quickly, her dark eyes bright.

Cleo walked quickly to the patient's bedside and checked the monitoring equipment, almost expecting to observe no departure from the normal beat. For the first time she had doubts about Angie Carruthers as a nurse. If she was prepared to let personal considerations affect her in such a way on a ward like this...

But in fact Mr Tandred's beat *was* increased in frequency, though not greatly.

'What medication is he on?' asked Cleo, biting her lip.

'Xylocard, intravenous, on admission—which was this afternoon,' Angie said promptly. 'And now quinidine orally.'

'Shouldn't that bring it to normal, then?' Cleo asked. After all, Angie had been working on this ward for longer than she had.

'Yes...I wish Sister was back,' Angie said, then quickly: 'I think I'd better call Dr Fitzgerald.'

It *was* what she had wanted to do all along, and she was exaggerating her anxiety over the man's condition, and looking for support from Cleo, so that if Sister objected when she returned, Angie wouldn't stand for blame alone.

...Unless Cleo's feelings were clouding her judgment entirely these days. With a sinking heart, she knew that Staff Nurse Carruthers was not the only one who could be accused of bringing personal matters on to the ward.

'Yes, call him,' she said quietly at last.

With a satisfied look seeping through her carefully composed expression of concern, Angie went to the nurses' station to ring through for the Registrar. Sitting relatively close by while she recorded the most recent set of observations of her own patient's pulse, blood pressure, etc., Cleo could overhear snatches of Angie's words.

'In Casualty—I see. Well, could he be called anyway?... A message. All right.' She gave details of the problem, then waited for some moments. 'He can't come at all? Yes, but I'm still worried... Well, later if he possibly can... Yes, all right. In that case I'll let you know. Thank you.'

She hung up the phone and went back to her patient's bedside, looking disappointed. Evidently Tony hadn't been able to tear himself away from Casualty, and hadn't thought the problem serious, although apparently Angie had still insisted that he be asked to come to the Coronary Care Unit later if he could. Surely he would be angry at having to make the journey on such slim grounds?

But no, of course not. He was as interested in Angie as she was in him, and would only be glad of the excuse to chat with her, even briefly and in the hushed atmosphere of the ward. Cleo wished impatiently and angrily that the pair would get this preliminary skirmishing over and done with, and start going out together properly in their spare time. That would save everyone else from having to put up with the side-effects of their flirtation!

The red door-light on the desk lit up at that moment, and Cleo pressed the button to open the door. Sister Grieve was back from her late break, and clearly in a hurry. She came straight to Cleo at the nurses' station.

'Three people have just been brought in from a bad car smash,' she said, adjusting the cap on her greying high-piled hair with firm plump fingers. 'I heard on my way through the foyer. Switch was just about to page through to here. Intensive Care is pushed to the limit and now there's an emergency coronary as well. It's been decided that we're going to take him as we're quiet tonight, so I'm going to have to re-allocate staff.'

'Yes, Sister.' Cleo was alert immediately, personal problems pushed well to one side.

'I'll take the emergency, and I'll move Staff Nurse Carruthers to my patient in the next bed. That way we can help each other as the need arises. You'll take Mr Tandred as well as...'

'Mr Potter,' Cleo nodded.

'Mr Potter, who you're with now. They're both well settled with no problems, aren't they?'

'Yes, except...'

'Here's the admission now.' Sister Grieve reached quickly across to respond to the red door-light before Cleo could explain what had happened with Mr Tandred during her absence, but perhaps after all it didn't need to be reported. Tony hadn't seen the need to come—although that might be purely because he was up to his neck working over the three accident victims who had just been brought in.

Still, there was no time to worry about

the matter now. Sister Grieve and Angie were already fully involved with the new patient, Graham Reeves, who would need scrupulous attention if he were to survive. Probably an extra nurse would be put on for the night shift, which was due to commence in a few hours.

Cleo now had responsibility for two patients, which meant a lot of extra work, so she set about the task of skimming rapidly but carefully through Mr Tandred's notes, charts and observations in order to be as familiar as possible with his condition.

It was an hour before there was any time to draw breath on the ward. On glancing about her, Cleo was amazed that the other patients seemed so undisturbed by the new arrival, but she realised that everyone, including herself, had kept their sense of urgency under tight control, speaking only in murmurs, and treading lightly and silently even though they hurried back and forth through the ward.

For a short while, the emergency admission's life had hung precariously in the balance and a doctor—an older man whom Cleo did not know—had hung over him, issuing curt instructions and seeming to keep the man's heart beating through sheer force of will. He had left now, medication had been given, and the rhythmic movement of light on the monitor was steady.

Cleo would remain busy for another two hours, juggling her double load of monitoring procedures and other aspects of patient care. When the admission light flared red on the desk again, she scarcely thought about it, but pressed the button mechanically and went back to work. Probably the unknown doctor returning to check on his patient again.

'I was called up here earlier in the evening. Is everything all right now?'

Cleo looked up from her desk. It was Tony. This was the first time she had seen him since his return from Edinburgh. He looked exhausted, the cast of shadows in the dimly-lit ward exaggerating this impression. No doubt it was the result of his heavy night in Casualty.

'Yes, it was Mr Tandred,' Cleo explained, picking up the patient's charts and moving quietly across the floor to Angie's former patient, who was now asleep. Tony followed her.

'I got a message that the frequency of his ectopic beat was high,' he said. 'The medication should have brought it back to near normal.'

'Yes, quinidine, orally, and...'

'I was told you'd ring through again when you were no longer concerned, but when I'd finished in Cas. Switch said there was no message, so I came up. What's wrong? Has there been no change?'

He spoke rapidly, clearly eager to solve the problem as soon as possible so he could go to his no doubt well-earned rest. Cleo bit her lip.

'Actually, it's fine now,' she told him, steeling herself against her awareness of his faint male scent that reached her across the small distance that separated them. 'You see, we...'

'Then why didn't you leave a message with Switch as you were supposed to do?'

The words were quietly spoken but with whiplash force that almost had Cleo reeling. Could it just be tiredness and irritation over this mistake that made him so angry? It was unlike the Tony she had come to know and burned with care for.

Suddenly she was angry too. He had attacked her before giving her a chance to explain. And the fault had been Angie's, largely.

'I was about to explain,' she said coldly. A glance at his eyes had revealed that they were glazed over with the impersonal regard of a stranger.

Something's happened, she thought. Something's made him change his mind about me again. It's not even indifference and a bit of physical attraction now, it's downright dislike. Had Angie told him some story? Or Shirley! What could it be? But he was waiting for her explanation.

'It was Angie—Staff Nurse Carruthers—who paged you,' she explained. 'Mr Tandred was originally her patient, but we had an emergency admission. Angie was transferred to the other side of the ward, as you can see, and forgot to tell me I was supposed to ring through if Mr Tandred's condition improved.'

'Oh, it was Angie...' His face changed suddenly.

Cleo's heart lurched painfully and her throat constricted. Without stopping to consider the consequences, she spoke her thoughts aloud.

'Yes, that makes a difference, doesn't it? The fact that it was Angie and not me. Do you think it's right to carry personal feelings on to the ward like that?'

There was a discernible pause before he spoke, and Cleo waited with tight lungs, as if for an explosion. When he did reply, the quiet words came as a surprise.

'No, it's not right,' he said, his eyes narrowed but steady. 'Don't worry, it won't happen again.' Then his tone changed to become a drawl that seemed to disguise at least part of what he was thinking. 'But perhaps you should consider whether you've behaved irreproachably yourself.

258

Isn't there a saying or two to that effect? People in glasshouses...'

Before she could start to wonder what he meant by the accusation, he had left her and gone to the other side of the ward. To Angie, of course, and Sister Grieve, who both hovered around the emergency admission's bedside, as well as monitoring the progress of Sister Grieve's other patient.

The three of them exchanged some low words and Tony examined the new patient's notes. Then he gave a polite good night to Sister and exchanged what looked like a very special smile with Angie—though admittedly, his back was to Cleo and she could only see the pretty nurse's face indistinctly in the lowered bluish lights of the ward.

A moment later the ward door had sighed and clicked and he was gone. Cleo glanced at her watch. A quarter to eleven. Not too much longer till night staff arrived, but she felt the time would pass very slowly in spite of all there was to do.

'Staff Nurse Fitzpatrick?' Night Sister Helen Winters, a creamy-skinned redhead in her late twenties, skimmed up to Cleo with a rueful smile as soon as she arrived.

The two had not met before, as Sister Winters was new to the hospital, but Cleo had heard of her. Only recently married, she was putting up with an introductory stint of ten weeks' night duty with a generous lack of complaint, and word had gone round that she was marvellous.

'Yes, Sister Winters.'

'Look, you're going to hate me,' she said. 'We haven't been able to get an extra nurse for this shift and we can't manage with three, with the new admission. I'm asking you to stay on for a double.'

Her rueful smile was now explained. Cleo felt ready to drop at the very thought of being here throughout the long night, but she knew there was really no choice. And the large grey eyes of Sister Winters were very hard to rebuff.

'Of course I'll stay.'

In fact, in the end, the extra hours of duty were not so hard. Through sheer determination, Cleo summoned an extra spurt of energy and alertness, helped by cups of coffee or tea at intervals, as well as—aided and abetted by Helen Winters—the shameless raiding of Sir Phineas Grimes's special biscuit tin.

The new patient, Graham Reeves, continued in a stable condition, and none of the other patients gave cause for alarm. Every now and then, Cleo had time to wonder about the meaning behind Tony's unexpected and powerful accusations, but her weary mind could find no answer to the problem, and she knew it would have to wait until sleep had sharpened her intelligence again.

It was after eight the next morning when she arrived home, having taken a taxi from the hospital. Jane was up and dressed and hopping about the kitchen with a bright-faced energy that Cleo could only envy. For once it was sunny, and a shaft of bright light beamed warmly into the kitchen, lending a glow to the glaze of pottery bowls and the glass on a still-life print of autumn-toned flowers.

'I heard what happened, you poor thing,' was Jane's greeting. 'And I guessed you had to stay on. They couldn't get extra night staff to cover the emergency, right?'

'Right,' Cleo nodded.

'And, although ready to drop, you're also starving, right again?'

'Right again.'

'Well, don't worry, 'cos look! Da-dah!' With a magician-like flourish, she produced a large plate from the warming drawer, added a generous dollop of cooked tomatoes to the piece of toast that sat on it, beside a rasher of crisply-grilled bacon, and set it down on the table in front of Cleo. The hot savoury aromas had her mouth watering instantly.

'Oh, Jane, you are an angel!' Impulsively,

Cleo clung to her friend for a moment, then eased her tired muscles into a chair.

With a pang of guilt, she realised that lately there had been a tinge of distance and resentment in her feelings about Jane, simply because of her own feeling that Tony Fitzgerald was a subject that they couldn't discuss together.

'I've condemned her without a trial,' she realised. 'I've said nothing at all about Tony, then been upset because I thought she didn't care.'

And now Jane had got up early specially to prepare this wonderful breakfast. What was more, it seemed there were further delights in store.

'Here's fresh orange juice,' Jane was saying. 'And you can have tea or coffee or whatever you like. And I'm making pancakes with lemon and sugar to finish.'

'Oh, Jane! It's...'

'Don't tell me it's fattening! You need it!'

'I wasn't going to say fattening. I was going to say "too good to be true",' Cleo retorted.

'Hmm. Better wait till the pancakes are actually cooked before you get too excited,' Jane advised. 'I do sometimes make a terrible mess with them. They end up looking like scraps of torn sock.'

'I don't care what they look like,' Cleo said. 'I'll eat them with my eyes shut and I'm sure they'll taste fabulous.'

Fortunately for Cleo's appetite and chef Jane's feelings, it wasn't till the last mouthful of pancake had disappeared that Jane suddenly remembered something.

'Oh, I forgot to tell you!' The exclamation followed a contented silence broken only by sounds of sipping and chewing. 'Tony Fitzgerald, of all people, dropped round yesterday afternoon, just after you left to go shopping on your way to work.'

'Did he really?' Cleo kept her voice as expressionless as she could. The room suddenly seemed dimmer, and she realised it was because the sun had disappeared behind a cloud.

'Yes, aren't you surprised? When you detest him so much, I mean. I wouldn't have thought you'd given him much encouragement to come and visit you.'

'Encouragement?'

'Yes. At least, I assumed that was why he had come...' Funny Jane. Now that she was in love, she expected everyone else to be interested in the same thing. '...Even though you'd said it was Angie he was involved with. He didn't offer any other reason for his visit.'

'So...what happened? What did you say to him?' asked Cleo, somewhat listlessly.

After all, it could scarcely matter now, one way or the other.

'Well, you'll be really pleased—I hope,' Jane giggled wickedly. 'I knew you'd want me to put him off, so I told him you were on the verge of getting engaged—to a policeman!'

'A *policeman?*'

'Yes, I thought it added a certain extra element of deterrent. I said you'd been going out together quite seriously since last year. Bill Craddock, I said his name was—but perhaps that was going a bit far,' she added, as she noticed Cleo's face, which she had given up trying to hold in the right expression.

This accounted for last night's angry words from Tony. He believed now that the mythical 'Bill' had been in the picture from the beginning, which did put Cleo's behaviour in an unpleasant light. It made it seem as if she had deliberately said nothing about her supposed involvement during the time she had spent with Tony in France, encouraging him to think that she was unattached, responding to his kiss, and then not replying to his two cards.

A man like Tony, who had pride as well as a strong measure of integrity, would not take kindly to being deceived and trifled with. Cleo doubted that he was hurt—there was Angie, after all—but she knew he was angry, and guessed she had lost any chance she might have had left of gaining either his interest or his friendship.

'Cleo, have I done something terrible?' Her friend's silence had become too noticeable for Jane to ignore it any longer.

'No, it's my fault,' Cleo said tiredly. A spattering of rain cut across the end of her sentence. The fine morning had been a fickle one. 'I should have told you long ago, but...anyway. You see, Tony Fitzgerald and I spent a week together in the same hospital in France.'

The whole story was told in detail, and to her credit Jane took the revelation in her stride like the true friend she was, asking concerned questions every now and then, but letting Cleo reveal everything in her own way.

It was only at the end that she started to display an attitude whose optimism only depressed Cleo further.

'Well, what are we going to do about it, then?' was Jane's question.

'Do?' queried Cleo.

'Yes. I mean, we must have a strategy...'

'For what?' Cleo didn't even try to keep the weariness out of her tone.

'For making it clear that it was all a mistake or a misunderstanding. You're not

265

going to take it lying down, are you?'

'Jane, I don't see what else I can do!'

'Rubbish! Sorry, love, but you've got to be *assertive!* It's the in thing, everybody's reading books about it.' Jane galloped off on one of her pet hobbyhorses. 'I mean, eight months ago David didn't know I existed, and now we're engaged, so you see.'

'Engaged!'

'Oh, damn!' Jane's small freckle-dappled features were suddenly suffused with pink. 'I didn't mean to tell it to you like that. I was going to pick my moment so carefully, but I got carried away, as usual, like the idiot I am—and we're supposed to be talking about Tony Fitzgerald.'

'There's nothing more to say about Tony,' Cleo said gently. She was relieved, actually, that Jane's rhetoric had swept her off on to the unexpected track.

Now that Cleo had told her story, there really wasn't any point in dwelling on it, and she just couldn't share Jane's view that there was anything she could 'do' about it, with Angie so strongly in the picture these days. It seemed easier, instead, to encourage Jane in her happiness—not that much encouragement seemed necessary. The girl was positively glowing.

'That's fabulous,' Cleo said sincerely.

'You're perfect for each other, and I know you'll be happy. Have you set a date?'

'Not exactly,' said Jane. 'But there seems no point in waiting too long. Maybe September.'

September! Less than three months away. With a sick pang, Cleo realised how much the event would affect her own life. David lived in a tiny place, quite unsuitable for two, whereas through a fortuitous arrangement, Jane had this lovely flat for the next three years. It would be perfect for a newly-married couple, but where did a third person—herself—fit in?

Of course Jane wouldn't turf her out. In fact, she'd probably beg her to stay till Aunt Louise's diplomat friend returned from her posting and they all had to leave, but Cleo wasn't inconsiderate enough to play gooseberry like that.

When Jane got married and David moved in, Cleo would have to move out, and that almost certainly meant back to the nurses' home. Unless she simply swapped with David, which might not be *too* bad, although according to Jane, the bathroom smelled badly and incurably of damp...

Jane was still talking almost shyly about their plans, and Cleo guiltily returned her attention to the subject. Had Jane noticed that her mind had wandered?

'...So we're planning a bit of a celebration. Nothing very big, just a picnic the Saturday after next. Are you free? Do you want to come?'

'Don't you two want to be alone?' Cleo summoned a smile.

'Heavens, no! We can be alone any time we like. Anyway, as I was about to explain, some people have rigged up a social tennis tournament, with some ex-fellow med. students at Cambridge. David's been conned into the men's doubles with Chris Caird—he's from Obstets., you probably don't know him. We thought we'd drive over in the morning, have lunch, do the tennis bit, then follow on with whatever activities the others come up with. Now, are you working?'

'I'm not sure, but if I'm not, then...'

'Then you absolutely have to come, because I care a lot about you, Miss Fitzpatrick, and I'm worried about you.'

'I'll check my roster,' promised Cleo.

'Do that, and then straight away go and get some sleep!'

Cleo sighed and laughed and sighed again. She was very tired. And when Jane got schoolteacherish, it was usually sensible to obey.

CHAPTER ELEVEN

Cleo was woken on Saturday morning by a veritable orchestra of birds outside her window, and by the dancing patterns of leaves and sunlight projected against her cream curtains. It was the first glimpse of sunshine London had seen since the morning Jane had made breakfast for her—now a week and a half ago. The bright start to the day seemed like a good omen, but perhaps it would prove as shortlived as the last one had been.

For a moment Cleo was tempted to turn her back on omens of any kind and hide again in sleep, but this was a special day for Jane and so she had a duty to begin it as cheerfully as she could.

The ten days that had passed since Jane's confession that she was engaged had not been easy ones. Cleo had spent most of them at work, both on early and late shifts, and Tony had appeared frequently.

Cleo would be bent over her work—either notes at the nurses' station, or direct patient care at the bedside—she would look up for a moment, and there he would be, swinging open the door to enter the ward, his footsteps quiet but brisk. Or sometimes he would already have entered without her noticing, and would be immersed in consultation with Sister, or in issuing instructions to one of the other nurses.

Twice she had been in the tiny ward kitchen when he had arrived. The first she had known of it was the faint timbre of his voice with the provincial accent that distinguished him from every other doctor at the hospital. She could always recognise it easily now, even above the singing of the electric kettle as she boiled water for coffee.

On both of these occasions he'd appeared suddenly in the doorway, nearly filling its frame, and then had abruptly moved away again after a few quick words that could only be lame excuses: 'No coffee for me, thanks, Staff,' and 'Sorry, I thought you were Sister.'

It couldn't be coincidence that on the two days when this had occurred, Angie Carruthers had also been absent from the main ward at the time. It was fairly clear to Cleo what was going on, therefore. Tony had finished his task on the ward, had heard footsteps and clinking coming from the kitchen, and had looked in, hoping it was Angie in there so he could exchange a quick word—or even a kiss—with the pretty, dark-haired nurse.

Cleo had easily been able to read disappointment in his quickly frozen features, and dislike and embarrassment in the way he wheeled around in the very doorway and couldn't be gone fast enough. Once—it was Wednesday evening—she had had to bite back a word, 'Wait!' because it seemed impossible that they could go on like this without some sort of discussion to clear the air.

And yet what was there to say? she wondered as she lay back on her pillows, comforting smooth things that they were, and stared unseeingly at the light patterns playing on the ceiling. Everything was quite clear without words. Wasn't one picture supposed to be worth a thousand of them?

Well, she had her pictures—Angie and Tony laughing together amongst a group in the dining-hall at mealtimes; Tony's blank, bland expression and cool impersonal eyes as he discussed a patient's condition and treatment with herself—'Mention that to Sir Phineas, will you, Staff?'; and Angie and Tony standing closer together than was strictly necessary as they consulted a patient's chart.

They were an artist's study in contrasts, with her dark hair and pale, creamy skin, and his fine, wayward jet-black thatch set

271

against a tan that was only just fading after Italy. The shape of their bodies seemed to fit too—Angie's slender curves and Tony's athletic, big-boned planes.

And as for words, what more conclusive verbal proof did she need than overhearing a snatch of their conversation as she passed their table in the dining-hall only yesterday.

Tony's deep voice with its well-defined consonants talking to two friends:

'...That moment when you first realise he's informing on the other guy!' And Angie, adding her bit to the conversation, clear-toned and enthusiastic: 'Yes, it was a fabulous film, wasn't it? I could actually feel your suspense, Tony, across the seat. It was long—we didn't get back to Tony's till really late, did we, Tony?—but I wasn't bored for a second of it.'

At that point Cleo had passed out of earshot, but she had heard enough. They were going out together, and going 'back to Tony's' afterwards. For a moment it was humiliating just to think of walking past them when they were now a couple and she was alone, but then she remembered Bill Craddock, the mythical policeman to whom she was supposedly engaged.

Now that Jane had conjured him into existence, he was a comforting sort of fellow. At least if Tony ever spared a thought for her, he would think she spent her time off nestled in 'Bill's' arms, rather than knowing she dreamed hopelessly of *him*.

'Cleo, are you awake yet?' It was Jane, tapping politely at the door.

'On the point of springing out of bed,' Cleo called back brightly. She'd vowed not to stay lying in bed, and now here she still was. 'It looks like a glorious day.'

'It is. Just a few little clouds bobbing about that look like flocks of woolly lambs,' said Jane.

'Oh my! Aren't we poetic this morning!' Cleo teased.

Since the door was still closed, she couldn't see Jane's satisfied expression at this evidence of rallying spirits, nor could she know that her friend had one or two undivulged plans afoot for the day. Perhaps, as regarded the latter, it was just as well.

David arrived with his car and his contribution to the picnic fare—fruit juice, champagne and cold meats—just as the girls finished clearing away the breakfast things. Jane had spent the previous morning preparing salads, and had been out into the early sunshine today to purchase bread and cheese. Cleo felt like a bit of a free-loader both because she hadn't contributed to any of this, and because, try as they might to

273

include her, Jane and David couldn't help being cocooned in a loving world of their own that would have left any third person a little out in the cold.

Still, Cleo reminded herself, it was their day, and it was only a matter of bad timing that stopped her from enjoying the sight of their happiness together, their engagement coming as it did just as she was finally realising that her love for Tony would have to wither before it had even fully flowered within her.

While the pair canoodled in the kitchen over the picnic baskets, Cleo crept up to her room and then out to David's car with the cake she had bought yesterday to present as a lunchtime surprise. In the front garden, the air struck warmly on her face and she realised that it was going to be quite hot as well as sunny, making sense of the breezy cotton dress she had chosen to wear.

This was its first airing, as she had bought it only recently, attracted by the bold abstract, floral pattern in different blues on a cream background. The skirt fell in smooth folds from a loose-fitting gathered waist, and the wide round neck and armholes revealed her lightly tanned collarbone and shoulders.

At the moment, a matching jacket in cream linen protected her arms against a morning chill that still lingered in the shade, but later they would be bare, and a fine gold necklace of plaited chain would twinkle in the sun. Tortoiseshell combs scraped her golden-blonde hair back over each ear, where it then fell loosely in a bouncing bob, behind slim, dangling gold earrings, and a light touch of make-up lent an added freshness of colour to her face.

Although Cleo did not realise it, out here in the sun, her new-found beauty was at its most compelling height, and no one would have guessed that the light-footed girl who slid a white cardboard cake-box carefully under a rug on the back seat of David's car was inwardly wondering if she would get through the day without crying.

'Oh, you're out here already, Cleo,' said Jane, appearing around the side of the house.

'Yes, is there anything else that needs to be brought?' she improvised quickly, enjoying a childish pleasure in keeping the gooey strawberry and cream sponge cake a secret until the last possible moment.

'No, we've got both baskets, and the Thermos and all that, haven't we, David?' Jane said.

'Yes, I can't think of anything else,' the physio responded cheerfully, his curls as bright as gold in the sun. Cleo saw Jane turn back and give an adoring glance, then stop to rumple the curls with loving fingers.

'I'd better just get my bag, then,' said Cleo. 'And I'll lock up on my way out, shall I?'

But they hadn't heard.

The drive to Cambridge was fun. Although it wasn't long since Cleo had been away from London to visit her parents in Devon, it felt very good to get away into quieter, more open spaces. The weather in Devon had been atrocious, and most of the time had been spent indoors, helping her mother with various craft and household activities. One windy, rainy walk with her father hadn't been enough to clear the hospital and the city from Cleo's soul, but today should be different, a complete escape, even though of course there were hospital people involved in the tennis tournament, she remembered.

'Who's playing?' she asked, half hoping they would all be strangers from one of the many domains of the hospital where Cleo's work never took her. Perhaps it might be nice to meet some new people.

'A couple that you'll know,' David began, but then Jane cut in.

'It wasn't decided finally, was it, David? Didn't one or two drop out at short notice and have to be replaced?'

'Oh...er...yes, so they did,' David nodded

quickly. 'I'd forgotten.'

Cleo smiled to herself. It sounded as if Jane regarded at least one of the players as an eligible man for her friend, but typically she was keeping this opinion elaborately secret so as not to spoil anything.

It was a trick she had tried before in the past, with the best of eager intentions, but without success. Would life go on like this for Cleo until it became quite pitiful? A series of ageing and frumpish bachelors being lined up ever-hopefully by Jane for an ageing and frumpish Cleo?

'Did I tell you you look fabulous today?' Jane turned abruptly to the back seat, catching the tail-end of her friend's expression.

'No, you didn't.'

'Well, you do, so keep it in mind.'

And Cleo, feeling the influence of the verdant countryside that was appearing now between the houses, knew she was going to be happy, at least for today. She owed it to Jane and David, and she owed it to herself. In a strange way she even owed it to Tony, because none of this mess was really his fault. If she could just shake off this feeling that he was a permanent ache living inside her, just shake it off for today, then perhaps she would be all right.

'It's a glorious day for an engagement celebration,' she said.

The backdrop of the river where David laid the woolly tartan picnic rug was a composition in different greens—the bright mirky shade of the water, the living translucent chartreuse and lime of leaves, and the darker oaky greens of distant shaded trees.

Out of London, one's sense of smell, jaded by petrol fumes and hospital disinfectant, suddenly came alive again. Cleo drank in mossy, woody odours and the sweeter scents of flowers carried to where they sat by a breeze that came in lazy puffs just often enough to keep the sun from becoming too hot on arms and neck.

Cleo's healthy outdoor appetite reminded her that she hadn't been eating particularly well over the past couple of weeks, and it was a welcome change today to enjoy every mouthful of the picnic meal. The strawberry cream sponge had been received with frank expressions of greedy delight by Jane and David. He had uncorked the champagne with endearing clumsiness, and when he had filled the glasses they had brought, he produced another surprise—a small crimson velvet box.

'Guess what, gorgeous!'

'The ring!'

'It was ready ahead of schedule. I picked it up yesterday.'

That had been Jane's one disappointment

278

ten days ago, that the ring she chose had had to be ordered and wasn't expected to arrive for at least two weeks. The modest diamond sparkled as she put it on, matching the tears that had suddenly pearled in Cleo's eyes. It was good to see Jane this happy.

Unsurprisingly, they were the last to arrive at the twin grass courts where the social tournament was to be held. David went ahead and disappeared into a green-painted club-house to don white tennis gear, while Jane and Cleo looked around to see where the other spectators would be sitting.

The courts were simple ones, with nothing spectacular in the way of seating arrangements, merely some white-painted slatted wooden seats which looked moderately comfortable.

There were about a dozen people seated there, a collection of bright, butterfly colours, as everyone had taken advantage of the warm day to blossom forth in summer fabrics. Two or three wore tennis whites, and were clearly about to participate in the game.

Cleo and Jane studied the group in search of people they knew from St Valentine's, but most of the spectators were strangers, and must be supporters of the local players. Only two people at the near end looked familiar to Cleo, and Jane murmured some information about them.

'Richard Palfrey from Gynae. He's not playing, obviously, but that's his girlfriend Jessica next to him in tennis gear. She's nice. In the social work department.'

Jane was walking up to the empty seats at the end as she spoke, and had got too close to go on with her explanations without it looking rude. She stood back to let Cleo take the first seat, and at that moment the nearest girl, who had been talking to Jessica, turned round and pulled off large sunglasses to give them a polish.

'Hullo, Cleo!' It was Angie Carruthers, bringing her inevitable reminder of a whole parcel of feelings that Cleo didn't want to think about today.

'Hi.' The word came out foolishly, accompanied by a wobbly smile and followed by a lame, 'I didn't know you were playing in this.'

Angie wore modishly flared and cuffed white shorts with a smart woven belt and a loose fashion T-shirt in aqua and white, that fell softly around her trim figure. An enormous floppy-brimmed hat had prevented recognition until she turned and took off her sunglasses, but now she exchanged this for a white sun-visor. The sporty little outfit set off her dark hair and creamy skin, and Cleo saw one of the Cambridge spectators, an owl-eyed young medical student, give more than one covertly admiring glance in her direction. Cleo was very glad that she at least felt well dressed today in her new bright-hued outfit.

'I got roped in by Jessica here, at the last moment,' Angie was saying. 'Yesterday, in fact. It was lucky I had a day off...and I think I'll be glad I came,' she finished, with a secret smile.

'Yes, because I don't know who else we could have got,' Jessica put in.

'This is Cleo, by the way,' said Angie. 'And... Sorry, I've forgotten. Isn't that terrible?'

'Jane.' The owner of that name supplied it cheerfully. 'But Jessica and I have met.'

'Chris had already asked several people after Eleanor Hastings pulled out on Wednesday,' Jessica went on. 'And then when he himself came down with 'flu on Thursday morning, we thought the whole thing might have to be cancelled.'

'So Chris isn't coming?' said Jane, sounding surprisingly disappointed.

She got on well with the young Resident, and so Cleo suspected that perhaps he had been the man that Jane had been planning to matchmake with her, and now her devious though of course good-hearted

281

schemes had been spoiled.

It was a pity, really, that Cleo had no interest in such things at the moment. Jane would have loved it if she could forget Tony Fitzgerald and fall in with a new proposition. Cleo wondered wearily how long it would be before she could, and suspected that it would be a horribly long time. But that was straying on to gloomy territory which she had promised herself to keep away from on this beautiful day.

To shake off the dangerous line of thought, she looked across to the clubhouse to see if the other players were emerging yet, and saw that they were—in a laughing group of four men and two women. The latter were Cambridge people, as were two of the men. Then there was David, of course, looking long-legged and energetic in his white gear, and lastly...Tony Fitzgerald.

Angie and Jessica got up with their tennis racquets and strolled over to the other players, to join the conference about who was to play whom. It did seem to be a very casual day, more a forgathering of old friends than a competitive match. Richard had moved away to talk to one of the Cambridge people now that Jessica was on the court, so Cleo could speak quite fiercely to Jane without risk of being overheard.

'Did you know Tony would be playing?'

Jane winced guiltily. 'Only since Thursday when Chris had to drop out.'

'Oh yes, of course you knew Chris had dropped out, didn't you? In spite of what you said before: "So Chris isn't coming?"' Cleo mimicked Jane's earlier performance of disappointment. 'Why didn't you tell me, and I would have stayed home!'

'Oh, Cleopotamus, are you really cross?'

'Yes, I am.'

Cleo stared down at the rolled grass. The teams appeared to have been fixed up now. On the court nearest to where they were sitting, there was to be a men's doubles, and Tony and David were already taking up their positions for a warm-up hit with two Cambridge players. Any second now he would see her, would think that she had come to see him, and her humiliation would be complete.

But before this could happen, Jane's fierce words brought her attention: 'Well, I'm cross with you. I knew you'd drop out if I told you Tony was coming and I wanted you to be here to celebrate with David and me. You can't avoid Tony like the bubonic plague for ever more—or are you going to resign from St Valentine's, renounce the world and go off to a convent in the jungles of South America?'

The question coaxed an unwilling laugh

from Cleo, which caught David's attention, and in turn, Tony's. The lanky physio blew a kiss across to Jane, while behind him Tony's face suddenly set after the briefest acknowledgment of Cleo's presence, and his eyes flicked away and he began to hit a ball across the net with one of the opposing players, sending low, punishing strokes time after time.

'Hey! I don't warm up as quickly as you,' the Cambridge player complained. 'Give us a break!'

'Sorry.' Tony changed his strokes to quick, short net-play and then some lazy loopy lobs that brought a laugh from the opposition and gave the impression that he had already forgotten Cleo's existence.

On the far court, the four women were enjoying their warm-up, and Angie's rather thin laugh broke out several times as she managed a fluke shot or missed a ball. Then there was a mix-up on the men's court, and all three balls ended up scudding into the wire fence behind the Cambridge players, creating a momentary lull.

'We're almost ready to start, aren't we?' asked a tall, green-eyed Cambridge man—Keith—while his partner retrieved the balls.

'I think so,' David nodded. 'What about you, Tony?'

'Ready when you are.'

Jane seized on the quiet moment to dart out on to the court and exchange a tiny good-luck kiss with her love. She also turned to Tony with a few short phrases. For a moment his face was blank as if he had not heard properly, then suddenly he grinned, shook his head and rumpled his dark hair in the gesture that always flipped Cleo's heart like a pancake.

What had Jane said to him? Evidently some wittily-worded form of good luck which had taken a moment to sink in.

'Yes, good luck from me too,' Cleo called impulsively, then wished she hadn't, because it meant that Tony looked over to her and smiled, and she had to meet his gaze, which seemed to have been fixed on her face for too long—part of that timeless element which so often entered into the air when Tony was around.

'Love-fifteen, good shot!' Angie's voice rang out clearly from the other court, breaking the odd, unexpected mood. The women's match had started already.

'Toss for serve?' queried Keith.

'All right,' replied Tony.

'Best of three sets, isn't it?' David asked. 'And then swap around for a mixed doubles.'

Then the game began. Tony was a very good player. In fact, the standard of play was generally high, and rally after rally consisted of hard, direct strokes hit with resonant clarity in the centre of each racquet head, then stinging the air with a hissing rush. It was exciting to watch, and the two pairs were evenly balanced at one set all when the four women finished their game, Angie and Jessica having won two straight sets.

'I'm hot,' announced Angie, plumping herself down beside Cleo. 'I'd just like to flake out somewhere, but I suppose I'd better lend my support to the home team.'

Cleo saw her hug in a secret smile and guessed that she had no intention of not watching the last thrilling set—or rather, watching Tony's athletic body as it moved around the court, with an expression of private possessive pride hovering about her pretty features. By now, Angie had probably held that sculpted body close to her own in long, sensuous embraces. She had probably run a lazy finger across the fine threads of black hair on his forearms, and had explored the hardness of each of those muscles that were now holding sway on the court.

An observant onlooker would probably find it comical, Cleo thought, the way she and Angie were sitting together, one girl openly watching her lover, and the other holding back her feelings and her gaze, trying to watch David or Keith or Max instead, trying to applaud each point impartially and watch the ball instead of one player's movements.

'Set and match. Well played,' said Keith, shaking Tony's hand after the final game had gone decisively Tony and David's way, ending the score at six-four, four-six, seven-five.

'Brilliant play, Tony!' Angie bounced up immediately, following Jane's lead. The latter, of course, had gone straight to David.

'Thanks.' Tony's reply was more casual and absent than Cleo, covertly observing, had expected it to be. Perhaps he was more reserved with his caresses in public than Angie, who had taken her cue from Jane's open, demonstrative affection. 'Are there drinks?'

'Yes, just lemon cordial between matches,' one of the Cambridge girls said.

This explained Tony's abstraction further; after the hot, punishing game, he was very thirsty. For about ten minutes, everybody milled around, chatting casually and downing large quantities of cordial. Cleo avoided Tony's eyes, knowing how transparent her own expression was bound to be, and of course he did not try to speak to her.

'So we'll have a mixed now, shall we?' said Keith, raising his voice. He seemed to be the chief organiser of the day, along with his Cambridge girlfriend Susannah, who had planned all the refreshments, but wasn't playing because of a sprained ankle. 'How shall we decide on the teams?'

'Well, I don't mind swapping courts,' said David. 'This one's in the shade a bit, and you lot must have been hot over on the other court before.'

'Were we ever!' Angie exclaimed, taking a cue quickly from this comment. 'And I must say, I would like a go in the shade. Are we keeping St Val's people together, versus you others?'

'It was supposed to be a fight to the death between enemy camps, yes,' Max put in with a laugh.

'Then I guess that means I play with Tony,' said Angie nonchalantly, brushing a dark lock of hair from her wide, smooth forehead and replacing her sun-visor. Cleo risked a quick glance at the Registrar. It didn't look as though he wanted to question the arrangement.

'Sounds okay to me. That means I'm with David,' Jessica said, and the Cambridge people quickly fixed up their teams. Max and a mousy-haired girl named Alice were to play opposite Tony and Angie, while Keith and Marie were opposing David and Jessica on the far sunny court.

'I'm going to watch David,' said Jane. 'But don't you come, Cleo. Stay in the shade.'

'Well, yes, I think I will.' She knew it was weak and foolish to want to stay here and watch Tony play, but she couldn't help it. Perversely, it would probably be good for her to watch Tony and Angie leaping about the court together, because perhaps it would eventually sink in that they were a couple once and for all, and there was nothing she could do about it.

This game was slower, but still exciting to watch. Cleo could see that Angie wasn't playing as well as she had in the women's game. She spent too much time watching Tony and standing back to give him room for an extra-powerful shot, and then wasn't in position ready for the next time she had to receive the ball.

'Sorry, my fault,' came out so often that it began to be irritating, and didn't Tony's 'No need to apologise' acquire a steely edge after a while? Perhaps theirs was a relationship of stormy arguments and rapturous makings-up, although from what Cleo knew of Tony—and she felt she knew him very well—that didn't seem like his style.

Halfway through the second set, it was

clear that Tony and Angie were going to lose, and Cleo's attention wandered a little. Over on the other course, Jane was still intent on David's performance. He and Jessica were playing well, and looked as if they would win comfortably.

'Forty-fifteen, match point,' said Alice, waiting for Max to retrieve Angie's ball, which had gone out over the base-line to give the Cambridge pair the point.

Max wound himself up for when he clearly hoped would be a final serve, seeming to hover immobile in the air for a moment before his racquet came down hard on the ball. It was an excellent serve, hitting forcefully against Tony's racquet. Max met the return powerfully too, and before the path of the ball could even be known, Angie had called to Tony 'Yours!' and stepped aside. He was moving forward but was taken by surprise at her call, and his shot, though hard and strong, deflected off the frame of his racquet and...

Cleo was just thinking how pretty Jane looked when she smiled at David, and what a difference love could make to a person's appearance, when Tony's ball hit her directly above the eye.

There was a chorus of gasps and a gut-wrenching sound from Tony. Cleo's vision went black and then was filled with exploding points of light, and almost immediately she felt the warm well of blood seeping through her eyebrow and down to her cheek. She felt weak, faint and green, and would have fallen forward off the seat if Tony had not reached her at that moment, scooping her into his arms and gently lifting her face.

'Cleo! My God! Oh, bloody hell!' he exclaimed, pithy ejaculations that might have brought a laugh from her at another time.

At another time, too, she would have been intensely aware of his cradling arms, his strong thighs and his firm, sculpted chest, all pressing against her. Now, however, she was reeling and needed his support, not caring that she fell against him with the whole weight of her body.

'Cleo, is it your eye? It wasn't your eye, was it? Oh please, my—' he bit back a word. 'Was it your eye?'

'I don't think so,' she managed to say. 'Above it. It's bleeding.'

'I can see that, precious. It's badly cut. It'll need stitches.'

'Take her to Cas.,' said Max. He named the hospital nearby where he himself worked. 'They run a pretty good department there. Got your car?'

'Yes.'

'Need anyone else to come?'

'No, not if Cleo can hold something

there to stop the bleeding. Can you, Cleo?'

'Yes, I'm sure I can.' She was recovering some composure now, could stand, and no longer felt she would burst into sobs in another second. Tony let her go, she'd actually be all right, but his nearness was so achingly sweet that she simply didn't have the strength to think beyond that.

'Lucky it happened on the last point,' Angie said flippantly, and there were a few scattered, short laughs.

'Don't wait for us,' said Tony. 'You came with Jane and David, didn't you, Cleo?'

'Yes.'

'I'll take you home. After all, we might be a while.' He shifted his position so that one capable arm stretched across her back and came around her, beneath her shoulder. 'Put your other arm around me. Can you walk to the car? You're not going to faint?'

'Not any more.'

'Good girl!'

They walked slowly to his car together, while Jane scampered to David's vehicle and got out Cleo's jacket and bag to transfer them to the low-slung blue sports model.

Expertly, Tony slid her into the seat, and from his bag of tennis gear produced a fluffy grass-green hand-towel, which it seemed a shame to see covered in blood. In fact Cleo hesitated for several seconds until Tony himself folded it into a wad and guided her hand with it to her forehead.

'There!'

Suddenly, as a drowning man sees images of his life, Cleo clearly saw, like a stiff photograph, the night of the hospital Christmas party, when she had doused his suit in beer and he had pressed away the damp with a wad of green paper table napkins held in his capable firm hand. Did she think for one moment that the same hand held against her own as he helped her with the towel would have such power to stir her senses?

While she still felt the phantom imprint of its pressure, Tony had left the passenger side and moved around to the driver's seat, starting the engine with a quick impatient gesture, and leaving it little time to warm up before pulling the wheel around and skidding out of the tennis court car-park in a scatter of gravel.

Again, Cleo had the impression that the onlookers in their tennis gear or pastel summer dresses and shirts were frozen like a photograph. Standing out in this photograph more than Jane's worried face and the Cambridge people's polite concern was the face of Angie Carruthers, frozen in disappointment and pique.

They didn't talk much in the car on the way to the hospital. Now that the initial buzz of activity had ceased, Cleo felt drained and dizzy again from the shock that was seeping into her frame. The green towel already felt warm and sticky against her hand and she knew she had lost a significant amount of blood. Professional instinct told her that the cut would need several stitches, and would not be a pleasant sight. She winced as she began to wonder about the likelihood of permanent scarring.

Half an hour later it was all over. Tony had waited outside, flipping unseeingly through magazines. It was a new experience for a man who was so often on the other side of the scene. A local anaesthetic quickly dulled the pain that was by this time throbbing badly in Cleo's forehead and temple, and after several stitches had been laced across the gash, and a neat dressing applied—which gave her something of a pirate's rakish look—she was assured that when the wound healed, only a thin line would mark the place where it had been. By the time she was released into the waiting-room where Tony sat, she felt like a new woman.

She saw him before he was aware of

her, a heavy frown creasing his usually smooth forehead, his hair a positive bush after the tennis and after he had run a hand through it a dozen times. Now his fingers were drumming nervously on the arm of his seat, and as she approached him, Cleo said the first thing that came into her head, quite without thinking.

'You look as tense as a new father in the early labour ward!'

He looked up with a quizzical smile, and she blushed hotly as she realised how her comment implied a closeness between them that did not exist. Of course he ignored the gaffe.

'How are you? Everything OK?'

'Miles better, thanks. Oh, I never noticed before—I've got blood all over your shirt. How horrible!'

The open-necked white sports shirt was indeed stained a messy rusty brown on one side of his chest, and she could remember now how she had let her head rest there weakly for several moments, deriving strength from the feel of his breathing and the warm male smell of his after-shave.

'It doesn't matter. It was an old shirt,' he smiled.

'Doesn't look old,' she retorted, but Tony only shrugged, then a wry expression passed across his even features. 'So...hadn't you better ring Bill and tell him what's happened?'

'*Bill?* Oh, Bill. But there's... Yes, perhaps I had.' Hastily Cleo recomposed her face into a look of what she hoped was loving anticipation. She had been on the point of saying that Bill didn't exist, but on second thoughts, at least he saved her pride in the face of Angie and Tony's new togetherness. 'I wonder where there's a phone...' she began.

'Cleo. You adorable girl!'

Without warning she was in his arms and his lips were pressing first into her golden hair, kissing it caressingly, then to her forehead, beside the clean new bandage, and then down to her flushed cheeks. Finally they came to her lips, uncaring of the other patients who waited restlessly for attention just yards away.

For some seconds Cleo responded fiercely to his kiss, feeling it stirring her senses to their depths and not stopping to wonder about what it meant, but then reason intruded, and she pulled away, with hurt mouth and narrowed eyes.

'You can't do this,' she said in a low voice, not caring about the betrayal of her love that she was about to make. 'It's happened before and it hurts me too much. You know how I feel about you, and you're just doing this when I'm too vulnerable to resist.' She willed herself to keep looking at him, demanding an answer from him with her anguished eyes and trying to ignore the fact that his arms were still around her, moulding her shape with soft firm movements.

'Darling, why do you need to be hurt?' he was saying. 'Don't you realise that I care about you? I know there's no such person as Bill-the-policeman—Jane has a mischievous imagination, doesn't she? She told me today, just before the match, and I spent the whole game longing for you between every point, and wondering when I'd get the chance to talk to you alone.'

'This isn't very alone,' Cleo said drily.

'No.' He glanced around him quickly. 'Perhaps you're right. Do you want to go?'

Before she could reply he pulled at her hand and they were out of the building and into the sun again.

'Where? What are we doing? Finish what you were saying,' said Cleo—illogically, since she had just finished objecting to the fact that these revelations were taking place so publicly. Her hand was small in his, but it seemed to fit there perfectly nonetheless.

'We're going punting.'

'Punting?' she queried.

'It's what one does at Cambridge, isn't

it?' he said. 'Generations of undergraduates have spent three years of their lives doing little else, according to popular myth.'

'Stop,' she said, beginning to believe in this sudden rush of happiness at last, but wanting to make sure. 'Kiss me again first.'

'In the car-park?'

'Yes,' she nodded wickedly. He did so. 'And finish telling me now?'

'If you like. Jane said you thought it was Angie I wanted.'

'Haven't you been going out with her?'

'Twice. In an attempt, which was entirely unsuccessful, I might say, to forget you.'

'I think she's rather keen, though, isn't she?' Cleo frowned.

'Oh no, not really. Angie's not ready to settle down yet—she told me so herself. But that's enough about her, don't you think?'

He kissed her again, playfully, on tip of nose and lobe of ear and the curve between her neck and shoulder.

'The first time I kissed you my hand was in plaster, and so was your leg, and now you're dressed up like Jack who broke his crown and had to be plastered in vinegar and brown paper. I hope it's not the start of a trend...'

'Tony,' she caressed his name with her mouth, like a sweet morsel. 'Was it because

I didn't write to you in Italy that all this has taken so long to come right?'

'Why *didn't* you write?' he wanted to know.

'I never got your postcards. At least, I got them about two weeks ago.'

'Two weeks ago! I wrote them months ago!'

'I know. They got lost in the post somehow, I presume...' It was pointless at this stage to bring poor mixed-up Shirley into the picture.

'Then that explains so much. When you didn't write, and when France seemed to recede so quickly into the past, I started thinking about how much you'd seemed to dislike me on the ward. Apart from that one time—do you remember?—with Mrs Weldon and her ninety-four Valentine cards.'

'Of course I remember. I felt that fate must be playing games with me. Working at St Valentine's Hospital, the Weldons and their cards, and then the two that Shirley sent us, supposedly from each other,' Cleo murmured.

'So it was Shirley Byrne?'

'Yes,' she bit her lip. 'I didn't mean to let it slip. It doesn't matter any more.'

'You mean Valentines are no longer of any importance at all...?'

'Not till next February.'

'But getting back to *last* February,' Tony said, some minutes later. 'France was like a different world. After a while I couldn't believe in it at all, and started to feel like a fool for having let it become so important.'

'It was the same for me,' she told him.

'And I decided you'd just been bored and lonely, and were indulging in a small holiday flirtation.'

'Which is exactly what I thought about you. And you have to admit, you did detest me when we first met.'

'Mere electricity, my darling.' His lips brushed hers again, and his arms tightened around her.

'But no, seriously...'

'I was fighting withdrawal symptoms after just kicking forty cigarettes a day,' he said. 'And I was working like fury. Fin Grimes was at me to go for my exams this year, when really I knew it was more sensible to wait.'

'Why is Sir Phineas so interested in you?' Cleo asked.

'Let's get in the car and I'll tell you as we drive.'

She did so, and treated herself to the sight of his face set in lazy concentration as he put the car in motion.

'What are you looking at, darling?' he asked.

'Just you.'

'In answer to your earlier question. It's all rather stupid really,' he grimaced. 'He's a great snob of a man. And in passing I have to tell you that I was as jealous as hell when I knew you'd been out with him, as well as anxious about you, because I knew he'd toss you over as soon as look at you.'

'I came to my senses and realised that too, before any damage was done,' she assured him.

'Anyway, he's a brilliant doctor, but a snob, as I said, and the idea of having me as a protégé appealed to him. He wanted to push me to the top of the tree as fast as he could, because it would reflect credit upon him to have advanced the career of young Sir Anthony.'

'*Sir* Anthony?' echoed Cleo.

'The fact is, my dear,' he smiled ruefully, 'I happen to be a baronet, in spite of this non-Etonian accent. Tedious, isn't it? My grandfather landed the title for war service, but meanwhile my father had settled in the North, without much money or much of a career, though he was a good man and a happy one, I think. My mother's a schoolteacher's daughter with no claims to illustrious ancestry. My father died some years ago, so the title passed to me. Sir Anthony Fitzgerald, second baronet.

I never use it, but people like Fin Grimes are impressed and think I should.'

'But he's a "Sir" himself.'

'Only a minor knighthood, darling, and one that he won't be able to pass on to his descendants.'

'Of course. How demeaning for him!'

'When I woke up to the fact that that was where his interest sprang from, I felt pretty cynical, and started to wonder why I was pushing myself just because he thought I should. That was why I decided on the holiday in Italy. Satisfied?'

'Completely.' Cleo remembered the night of her dinner with Fin and his angry and cryptic remark about Tony not using his full title. It made sense now.

'And I am too. Or will be, when I can kiss your pretty face again without that bandage.' Tony took a hand recklessly off the wheel and cupped it caressingly against her cheek.

An hour later, the bandage didn't seem to get in the way at all, and as they floated lazily together on the water, drifting slowly downstream, Cleo blessed minor accidents from the bottom of her heart—spilt beer, broken legs, strained brachial plexii, and gashed foreheads.

Then she started thinking about the Valentine's Day card she would give Tony next year.

The publishers hope that this book has given you enjoyable reading. Large Print Books are especially designed to be as easy to see and hold as possible. If you wish a complete list of our books, please ask at your local library or write directly to: Magna Large Print Books, Long Preston, North Yorkshire, BD23 4ND, England.

This Large Print Book for the Partially sighted, who cannot read normal print, is published under the auspices of

THE ULVERSCROFT FOUNDATION

THE ULVERSCROFT FOUNDATION

. . . we hope that you have enjoyed this Large Print Book. Please think for a moment about those people who have worse eyesight problems than you . . . and are unable to even read or enjoy Large Print, without great difficulty.

You can help them by sending a donation, large or small to:

**The Ulverscroft Foundation,
1, The Green, Bradgate Road,
Anstey, Leicestershire, LE7 7FU,
England.**
or request a copy of our brochure for more details.

The Foundation will use all your help to assist those people who are handicapped by various sight problems and need special attention.

Thank you very much for your help.